Desert Journey

a novel

CAROL MAY

TRAFFORD
CANADA • UK • IRELAND • USA • SPAIN

© Copyright 2004 Carol May Mahony.
All rights reserved. No part of this publication may be reproduced, stored in a retrieval system, or transmitted, in any form or by any means, electronic, mechanical, photocopying, recording, or otherwise, without the written prior permission of the author.

Note for Librarians: a cataloguing record for this book that includes Dewey Decimal Classification and US Library of Congress numbers is available from the Library and Archives of Canada. The complete cataloguing record can be obtained from their online database at:
www.collectionscanada.ca/amicus/index-e.html
ISBN 1-4120-3767-0
Printed in Victoria, BC, Canada

TRAFFORD

Offices in Canada, USA, Ireland, UK and Spain
This book was published *on-demand* in cooperation with Trafford Publishing. On-demand publishing is a unique process and service of making a book available for retail sale to the public taking advantage of on-demand manufacturing and Internet marketing. On-demand publishing includes promotions, retail sales, manufacturing, order fulfilment, accounting and collecting royalties on behalf of the author.
Book sales for North America and international:
Trafford Publishing, 6E–2333 Government St.,
Victoria, BC v8t 4p4 CANADA
phone 250 383 6864 (toll-free 1 888 232 4444)
fax 250 383 6804; email to orders@trafford.com
Book sales in Europe:
Trafford Publishing (uk) Ltd., Enterprise House, Wistaston Road Business Centre, Wistaston Road, Crewe, Cheshire cw2 7rp UNITED KINGDOM
phone 01270 251 396 (local rate 0845 230 9601)
facsimile 01270 254 983; orders.uk@trafford.com
Order online at:
www.trafford.com/robots/04-1595.html

10 9 8 7 6 5 4 3

in memory of
my father,
Arthur Adam

PART ONE
STARTING OUT

Something's happened to the order of time. For the life of me, I can't think how I've landed in such a dustbowl. A neon sign back down the road blinks "Oasis Resort"...but that can't be right. Underfoot are whorls and twigs of prickles and beside me, body-sized cactuses wave me on with their grotesque arms. Why am I shivering, in this searing heat? This isn't my place, that's for sure.

Where I belong, the cedars drip in curtains along the path to our cabin and the earth smells living at each footfall. Everywhere ferns spring up like giant bunches of feathers. Even the air smells green. When there's a gap in the forest there's always the possibility of mountains or ocean, and the birds mingle in each other's territory: the geese flying up from the beach over the treetops, the robins in branches overhanging the cliff calling to the sun as it rises from the sea.

But here only power poles mark a path... and where's it leading? It's all flat, so flat... except far in the distance, along the horizon. A faint, oddly familiar line of hills makes a pale blue variation. Maybe that's an illusion, one of those tricks of the dusty air that fools the crazed vagabonds in old cowboy movies. Or women suddenly alone, wondering how to survive.

8

A magpie has alighted on some barbed wire strung between two broken fence posts. It flicks its tail; I'm staring at the rhythm. It's a black and white Morse code: "go back, go back." The neon sign might be a new starting point. The sun's still low in the sky so the day has barely begun, but already it's out to dry up any living thing. Why have I still got my Chinese slippers on?

* * *

It was in the hotel...that's right. Early. (It seemed the middle of the night...jetlag I suppose). The sharp knocking on my door jolted me awake. It was a minute before I focused on Conrad in the bright hallway. He was beautifully put together as usual, suitcase in hand. I must have gaped dumbly, not even sure where we were – still in China? No, no this is the conference now, or was.

He wasn't in the mood for preamble. "My bus leaves in ten minutes."

My throat, dry, tried "What bus?"

"I've transferred the rental car into your name. The hotel bill is paid by the Association."

"Conrad..."

"No. Just leave it." His mouth barely moved, so set and controlled: his words and his anger.

I tried again. "Couldn't we talk? We haven't come all this way to just..."

He knew how to silence me with his narrow look of contempt.

"Marian. Forget it. It's too late for all that." And he turned away.

I grabbed my kimono and ran after him but he had his suitcase down the front steps before I could reach him. He strode out to the idling Greyhound bus. The driver stood by the door, tapping his foot.

"Wait, Conrad!" I ran toward him, but he turned on the step to give me that look, one more time. I felt the last threads holding us together stretch and break. He was gone in a blast of dust. Then the space in front of my eyes was empty.

* * *

Now I'm staring at the ignition. Hours must be ticking by. The notes from the conference are still lying on the dashboard, looking innocent now but implicated in all this. Renting the car was supposed to be for refreshing ourselves in America, after the muggy streets of Guangzhou. That first afternoon was like travelling together years ago. But that's all history now. This is hour one of a new kind of time, empty of Conrad. He's probably half-way to the airport by now, deleting me neatly from his life. Meanwhile, I'm left here in the desert to figure out why he couldn't stand another minute with me. And to find a way back home.

Ahead, the patch of parking lot and bougainvillea stretches out to nothing and maybe eventually, to the pale blue mountains. That's something to aim for. There's enough gas to last for awhile.

Driving in this blank landscape, it's becoming an illusion that I'm rolling forward. Really, it's "going back," as the magpie said. Back to my origin with Conrad.

We were thrown together then too, because we were both far from home. Back then, instead of the middle-aged comrade and mother that I am now, it was a naive girl who stumbled into London off the ship. The East End was a confusing din of double decker buses, voices with incomprehensible accents and footsteps rushing through the narrow space between brick buildings. This was far in every way from Herring Cove in British Columbia, where I was born.

All my family were originally from this "Old Country," though my sense of home was anchored in our village on the Pacific coast. I used to sit on the cliff watching the tide sliding in over our beach, while eagles and ravens called to me in familiar voices. Angled against the sky on the far end of our cove, totem poles quietly proclaimed the ancient clan figures: thunderbird, bear, dogfish, eagle, frog, raven. Sometimes my dad took me deep into the forest to visit the stone faces hidden under ferns. Secreted away in them were the stories of mythical times. They silently watched us. That's where I learned to love the damp, green places.

It was rare that we had visitors in Herring Cove. When a seaplane buzzed in, all the kids ran along the boardwalk to the dock to meet it. We were dying to find out who had come and if they had brought parcels from far away.

Now it was me in the far away, hailing a taxi for the first time, dizzied by the ride down Fleet Street and around Trafalgar Square until I was dumped with my dad's brown valise outside the hospital residence. It was straight from a Dickens' novel, with blackened brick, stone statues, tall dark windows and dim hallways. The austerity of my room seemed like the wartime that my father described. All around rumbled London, the centre of the world. I felt like a tiny tree frog in a huge concrete mansion. When I asked some nurses in the hallway where to start work, they had trouble understanding me, the Herring Cove accent was that foreign. They smiled as if to say, "Another Colonial, fresh off the boat."

September 14, 1967...the day I met Conrad. The first morning in the Royal Memorial Hospital I joined the line of therapists outside the dark panelled door of the Physiotherapy Department. They were chatting away about their flatmates, the shows in the West End, and joking with the only man in the group, Conrad. He stood tall above them, slender and straight, like a deer. His hair was curly and red then, and when he turned toward me, he smiled with gold-flecked eyes. Startled, I felt scared and new. He smiled with his eyebrows curving up, and came over to stand beside me. "Hi. You must be the new one. Let me show you around." His Canadian voice was the breath of home. For that instant I stood in an island of safety, looking up at him. As we shifted closer to Miss Hedley's office, the chat fell into undertones. He whispered, "Come along, Marian. Into the lair," and we entered the frosted glass room together. My palms were sweating and my neck was rubbed raw by the starched collar of the hospital tunic.

Miss Hedley's "right hand man," Gertrude Phynn, was the dragon behind the desk. Her narrow eyes summed me up with a glance.

"Ah, you must be the new Canadian. Uniform not up to standard, I see. Navy blue culottes here, not bright blue. And make an attempt at taming that fly-away hair of yours. Mr. Falk, be so good as to show Miss MacLean the department. A more formal orientation of the hospital will follow after tea this afternoon. Here is your patient list for today. And Mr. Falk, yours." Conrad deflected her scrutiny of me by leading me to Miss Hedley.

Our department head, seated in her armchair by the leaded glass windows, in dark blue blazer with a cluster of professional pins on her left lapel, extended her pale hand and murmured in a beautifully modulated English voice, "Welcome to the Royal,

Miss MacLean. We hope you'll enjoy your work here." Gertrude Phynn had levelled her cool gaze at Zerina, behind us.

Running after him as he strode down the hall to the physiotherapy rooms, I ventured, "Why is Gertrude Phynn so stern?"

"Undoubtedly the war, rehabilitating wounded soldiers. She's the lieutenant, giving the orders. Never call her Gertrude. It's Miss Phynn for the likes of us." (The sarcasm in his look was silent but eloquent.) "But don't worry, Marian. You'll be fine. She just doesn't like me. In the month I've been here, she already knows I see through her. She's got a lot to hide."

Naively, I dared to get too close. "Why?"

He edged away. Just a breath away. "It's complicated." Even then he chose his words carefully and never gave himself away: not blurting things out, or tongue-tied like me. That first day he took me under his wing and taught me how to cope, and I have to admit, dazzled me.

But I put on an ordinary face and my practical clinical voice and followed him to the treatment room. Khaki walls and grey floor were edged with parallel bars and a bank of high mats by the far windows. Standing on the mat, we could glimpse a narrow lane running below us faced by the stained brick walls and narrow paned windows of the hospital wards. Rooflines jagged with chimney pots indented the pale sky over South London. We sat on the high mat, which smelt faintly of urine and dust. Weights and pulleys, electrotherapy machines, and bolsters were lined up against the back wall.

Conrad leaned over me for a look at my list. "Oh, just a few for the morning, that's good. Rosalba Pereira: she's a sweet one, tends to talk your ear off. Your predecessor, Hilary, was always getting told off by Phynn for piling up the patients; the porters don't like it. They bring them from the wards every 45 minutes and if they get backed up it means they're late for lunch. Here's Mr. Boscombe. Come and meet him."

We crouched over an old man wrapped up with blankets in his wheelchair. His right forearm lay on a rolled towel in his lap. His head nodded gently forward, and a long arc of grey hair fell forward from his scalp and reached outwards of its own accord.

"Good morning, Mr. Boscombe, did you sleep well?"

He raised his head just enough to peer through his thick eyebrows. He smiled in a sloping line, the right side of his face refusing to lift. As Conrad smoothed his hair back, I noticed his amazing hands: long, almost balletic fingers and strong tendons under pale skin, the oblong nails bevelled and white. For a crazy moment I longed for that hand to be smoothing my hair, but I told myself how silly I was. Together we helped Mr. Boscombe pivot onto the mat for his exercises, and Conrad began moving his arm and leg in diagonal patterns, encouraging him to help with the action. A ray of sun fell on them, lighting up that glowing red hair. That's how we saw our first patient together.

He was right about Rosalba Pereira. She insisted I call her by her Christian name. "And I am Christian, doesn't that seem funny, but you know, I just went head over heels for Mr. Pereira and so I thought, well I'll always be mostly Hindu but what's the harm in embracing Mr. Pereira in every way, so you see I wear the cross just like him and now I don't suppose we'll ever have children and that's a good reason for being the same religion, but do you think my condition is in any way a punishment that God has refused Mr. Pereira this great blessing in life, you are new, aren't you? what delightful green eyes, where are you from, ah, so far from home, what does your mother think, such a big place, London, how to find your way? no, no, I cannot move my legs much today, sometimes you would be surprised, something down there wakes up for a little while, and I kick at the covers, I even laughed one day, "I'll dance again!" but never mind, I can think of those lovely parties, such beautiful frocks, my family wasn't strict, they wanted me to have fun, now I must have Mr. Pereira bring you something pretty, girls should decorate themselves especially in grey old London and with the winter coming on, but of course you know about the cold, you must be hardy, you won't be huddled over the electric fire like I was, singed my night dress so many times, Mr. Pereira used to say haven't I got enough fire for you, isn't he naughty, yes, the other girl tested my arms, my, you have strong hands for such a small person, she wrote it all down in her charts, she kept looking for my muscles to come back, I would think to myself, don't get excited, those days will not come back when I could reach out my beautiful arms to my husband with rows of shining bangles winking and singing to him... oh dear... but it is not wrong to cry, thank you my tissues are tucked into the pocket of my robe; do you like the colour? well yes, there is enough grey in this place, purple says something, thank you, you are a sweet girl."

She had one of those rare neuropathies, insidiously progressive. I helped her stand at the parallel bars by bracing her at the knees and holding her behind her shoulders, as in an embrace. Together we inched forward toward the mirror at the end of the bars. She laughed.

"Well, well! We are dancing after all! Who would have thought!"

I hugged her tighter. We turned and began our laborious return journey. For each step it was necessary to nudge her foot forward with my toes on her heel, and then quickly fix her knee with mine. As we settled into a rhythm, I glanced in the mirror. My face rested alongside her head. We were both not much more than five feet tall. My fuzzy pale hair puffed out beside her sleek black braid. I looked like a kid (which I was, I guess) with round face, red cheeks and freckles splashed across. My fingers clutching her purple dressing gown were small and dimpled and determined for this job. We made it back to her wheelchair, and she pecked me on the cheek, with winking conspiratorial eyes. A gem of a lady.

Everything stopped for morning coffee, with physios taking turns running to the kitchen for two big jugs, one of coffee and one of steamed milk, poured by a huge Jamaican woman surrounded by black stoves, and then teetering back to our staff room with the heavy tray. Miss Phynn would unlock the cupboard and set down the Windsor Castle tin of biscuits, the chocolate ones long gone. This kept us going, especially before payday.

Thinking back on it, the place was quite feudal: poor pay, with the various levels getting little perks according to their station. This was definitely in the style of the British Empire. Perhaps it was similar to Imperial China before the Revolution, with that strict hierarchy. Ah yes, the Earl's reception: Gainsborough paintings were brought out to grace the foyer, silver trays of Bristol Cream sherry were passed around among the benefactors and professors of neurology, respirology, cardiology, endocrinology. And in the doorways of the far recesses of the corridors stood the abler patients and staff like us, who practised apology, who accepted, or thought but didn't protest, all except Conrad.

"It's disgusting. Puffing them up so they'll give more money. Grand Rounds are almost as bad. Patients should not be subjected to that cold scrutiny. They're disoriented enough. Half of them wonder why they're even here. To be paraded into an amphitheatre, looked down on like an animal in a Roman Forum, and laid on a table as Exhibit A." His expression had the chilling power of a winter gale blowing into Herring Cove.

"But it's the same at home. It's so the professors can teach us."

"Demonstrating fancy tests: look! how this foot jumps or points or shakes –or doesn't, and pontificating on all the past cases, on and on while a real person lies there, made to feel like an entry in a medical journal, getting cold, having to pee but not daring to ask. And after, gratefully taking whatever new tablet the professor has decided upon. Disabled people shouldn't have to put up with that."

"But they say medical breakthroughs are being made here."

"Yes, and human beings lie in sheets too tight getting bedsores that become septic. That's a breakthrough too."

Even then I was in awe of him: he thought and spoke with such self-confidence. How had he leapt so quickly from being a humble student to a true professional?

Lunchtime gave us a chance to sit on a bench in the hospital square among the sweetness of the last English roses. Dusty sparrows hopped at our feet, in and out of the hospital's pointed shadow, while the London traffic roared outside our bower. It was odd: I felt safe with Conrad, even though he was quite remote. He was someone to want more of instead of fending off, like the guys I'd met up until now. He was almost like my leader, but neutral, giving me space to be myself.

When payday finally arrived, he suggested we go for a meal in the evening at "Mario's" on Red Lion Street. The waiter flourished us to a table for two by a window. Its leaded panes gave a rippled cast to the passers-by outside. Our table was spread with a red and white checked cloth and a candle stuck into a straw wine bottle so the wax dripped over and over in all the colours.

"What will you have, Marian? Veal scallopini? Some Chianti?"

"Conrad...do you do this all the time?" (This sort of meal was a first for me.)

"Don't get me wrong, Marian. I've hardly had a bean. But I did my training at McGill, and you can't help enjoying yourself a little when you live in Montreal."

He's pure sophistication. "Why come to London?"

"Well, you know...see the world, make some contacts."

"You mean with physio?"

"No, with guitar actually. I'm an aficionado of Julian Bream."

There's so much I don't know about. "Who's he?"

"Oh, a rising star, based here."

"Are you a guitarist too?"

"Oh, I dabble. At the moment I don't have a guitar. But next week there's a Bream concert at Wigmore Hall...Enough about me. Are you settled in yet? Got a flat?"

The candlelight defined his features with warm shadow. When he fixed his golden-eyed attention on me, I could hardly gather a phrase to answer him. "Well, not yet...they've let me stay in the hospital residence."

"Oh, good. Look, Zerina's friend Sarah may have a room in Earl's Court. You don't want to linger in that hole for long."

"Why?"

"You'll get your on-call rotation soon enough. Matron on Respiratory has decided we're worth having." He paused. "I offered round-the-clock respiratory treatment for intensive care chests, so you'll be given the big rattley alarm clock and Spartan quarters once a month. Unfortunately, our selfless service doesn't translate into more than our usual miniscule salary." He lapsed into silence, gazing out the window. A lurching group of young men burst from the pub across the street.

I watched Conrad – glamorous and impenetrable, and somehow self-sacrificing. I groped for a closer connection with him, perhaps a reciprocation.

I began, "Everything's different here: nothing seems normal to me. Even getting on the tube in the morning seems strange: people standing nose to ear, but isolated. The chat in the staff room seems in code. Is this culture shock? The patients are easier to be with...more basic. Wounded birds still singing the song of what they used to be, or quiet and waiting in a corner, just breathing."

He nods to me in slight amusement, but listening. I forge on.

"Speaking of patients, today I saw Mr. Dadson....you know, the lawyer from Ghana? His eyes were closed, thank goodness. It would be awful to move his arms and legs while he looks at his own paralysis. A woman visitor, maybe his wife, came in. She wore a high, brilliantly-coloured head wrap. She was very still, didn't speak to him, just looked, but her face seemed to collapse. I imagine he used to dress in a meticulous suit with a briefcase for his papers like the African men you see leaving the hotels near Russell Square in the morning. Probably he represented his country at negotiations, don't you think? His limbs are very heavy. They haven't atrophied yet. I found myself watching my white hands holding his black leg. I had to stabilize myself, one knee on the bed and lean in hard, to get full hip and knee flexion. Like heaving a big tree branch, with smooth black bark and hard strength underneath. Cast up, rare, on a grey shore. I started to sing to him, nursery rhymes of all things. But he's a mature man, with responsibilities and passions. Gone now, maybe forever, back into an infant state."

I clam up, a bit overcome. Foolish girl, blurting out all your feelings.

But no. Conrad, despite his self-containment, looked into my eyes with, I have to say, kindness. He reached across the table and gently took my hand from my wine glass. "Marian." Finally he said, "My new comrade." Acceptance: rare and heavenly.

After ward rounds the following week, I caught up with him in the hall. "Conrad, how was the concert?"

He lit up, literally glowed. "Superb! It was the Boccherini Quintet! Bream was marvellous!" His hands danced, describing the music, the hall, the audience. No restraint or understatement this time. We basked in this glow the rest of the morning, until we got to ICU.

Specific medical tyrannies forced our patients' lives into a mere struggle for breath. They'd once shopped at the corner store, washed their kids' faces and sent them off to play, wrote directives for their staff to act on, swung hammers in the street to build this city. Now they were reduced to the state where their names hardly mattered. This is what marshalled our energy, trying to restore their breath and their lives.

It's quite remarkable to realize how close we were then to the rudimentary beginnings of our profession. The other staff had procedures to do on the patients: nurses could medicate them, change dressings and IV's, wash and put salves on them; doctors could test and prescribe, or do surgery. But what could we do for them? All we had to offer were our hands, to move their wracked bodies till the day when they might move themselves. And our voices to motivate them to do something for themselves, even if only to breathe. We tried to find the spark that would bring their spirit into the fight. I felt like an interloper in the doctor-nurse territory, the "real medicine." Most didn't know what we did. It was that new. Conrad was determined that our profession have significance: moving and breathing –that was our territory. We puzzled out what to do. There was no technology, no monitors. The clues came by observation and the smallest changes in the old tried and true signs of heart rate, temperature, blood pressure. We borrowed stethoscopes to listen to the breathing, felt the quality and heat of the skin, and watched for flickers of expression in the faces. For most of the patients, the only functioning parts were above the neck: searching eyes, faint whispers, dry quivering lips.

"Mrs. Rowe, it's Miss MacLean. Good morning! I'm here to practise breathing. I'm going to turn you on your side. Which side would you like to be? Can you nod if it's alright? I'll vibrate your chest as you breathe out. I know it's difficult. *(Oh child, you can't possibly know)* Thank you for trying so hard, Mrs. Rowe. Rest now. *(Rest, rest. If only to rest)*."

The worst part was the suctioning with thin rubber tubes, of the sticky or frothy secretions from the lungs, while the patients heaved and gagged. And putting them on the respirators. A doctor after the war had contrived these primitive machines of pipes, bellows and motor that we dubbed "the vacuum cleaner." One day at ward rounds the head physician swept up to Mrs. Rowe's bed with Matron, the charts, and some Residents. We had her off the respirator, encouraging her independent breathing. But she was flushed and agitated, and we suctioned up some nasty yellow phlegm.

Dr. Lampton approached me sternly. "Well, young lady, what is your goal here... the patient looks very stressed."

Conrad jumped in to help me. "The point is to strengthen her breathing, Dr. Lampton. But she seems to have an infection."

"Hmm, let me have a look. You'd best leave her. The respirator will do the job."

"It's done a job all right. That old thing has probably given her the infection."

"Young man, that is gross impertinence. Your presence here is not as therapeutic as you imagine."

I know what Conrad wanted to retort: "We are trying to 'do no harm,' which is more than you can say for that contraption," but his angry flush said pretty much the same. Matron hurried the group to the next bed. But we got an earful later from Miss Phynn. We ran down the stairs at the end of the day, smarting from her rebuff.

"We don't belong here, Conrad. Maybe we just have to fit in with the system. We can't change anything."

"We're just at the beginning of what we can do. We need to speak out and push forward. We should be respected, not be pushed aside. Physio shouldn't be insulted. And those old ways have got to go. Chest treatment should be integrated; all the professions working together."

"What if the powerful professors don't want that?"

"Marian, I can't believe you'd fold up like that. Don't look so scared. We'll just have to get that good at what we do; then they won't be able to ignore us. They'll realize that we have a major contribution to make in restoring our patients to fully functional living."

He was right. I was taught in an all-girl class to regard the visiting male professors as having complete authority over our patients. "Following doctor's orders" is what we did, even though most had at best a vague notion of what physio entailed. Here in England it was the same system but with an even more military hierarchy. We literally stood to attention as the senior doctors conferred among themselves around the bedside of a befuddled, grateful patient. If a doctor shot me a darted query about the patient's condition, I almost froze with shyness. I stammered a few words which seemed to be ignored, and over and over I felt foolish and a nonentity.

It was much the same outside the hospital. Girls had to thread their way through a scary set of rules based on the authority of men. The crazy thing was that we learned to disapprove of ourselves and each other. Boys, of course, had quite a different climate to grow up in. That's why I was grateful to Conrad, for treating me like an equal colleague. He taught me to be a thinking professional who could receive respect for what I know, not a servant low down in a hierarchy.

The trick was not to pass the authority for my worthiness over to him. When doubt in my ability to help a patient weakened my resolve, I leaned on his irresistible confidence. He calmly analyzed each case, did his best, and then moved on. I had more trouble saying goodbye. My approach was to pour my heart into my patients' dilemma, rather like a daughter or mother. I believed that if I loved them enough, they would be persuaded to climb back up the ladder of health. It was a defeat when someone died or rejected the idea of rehabilitation. Conrad's more theoretical style was based on just as intense a dedication but more measured than mine.

I've often wondered, over all these years, what it was that Conrad saw in me. Perhaps it was that zeal of starting out, partners in our new profession. He seemed to be the leader, indulging and teaching me, but there was more to it than that. Sarah gave me a clue one day after work while we rode down in the elevator cage to the trains at Russell Square, the mechanical voice groaning, "Stand clear of the doors!" Her psychedelic pink earrings darted this way and that.

"I hear Conrad's leaving his room in Highgate. Do you know where he's going?"

"Oh, he's been invited to share a flat with someone he met at a concert – a guitarist." He'd told me that was the coda to his wonderful evening at Wigmore Hall.

"Now that's interesting. I thought he wanted to join us when Cecil leaves Earl's Court next month… I wouldn't be at all surprised if he wants to be nearer to you… you know."

(I was stunned. How could she know what he wanted?)

"Well, young thing, you're both quite transparent, you know. He stands to his full height when he's with you. It must be nice to be so adored. He needs that, doesn't he?"

As we dashed down the tunnel towards our platform, an eastbound train sent dusty gusts flapping at our maxi-coats. A pack of identical-looking school boys bumped by us onto the platform swinging their satchels at each other and pushing each other toward the line. As the light of our train advanced through the darkness, Sarah whispered, "In a weak moment when we were on call, he told me you're what he's missed all his life, but didn't know it! Now what do you think of that?… Hasn't he ever told you?"

We squeezed onto the train, pushed apart by expressionless raincoated men. Fortunately I was able to grab a strap to hold myself up; my legs felt like jelly. I wished he'd been the one to tell me…maybe one day he would. Hope, hope.

Conrad's new flat turned out to be near Clapham Junction, over the Thames, within walking distance of the big Arts Centre. He didn't talk about his new room-mate, or have time to go out for supper any more. Occasionally we treated ourselves to lunch at the pub, since it was far too cold now to sit in the square.

Then at coffee time one morning, he rushed over to me, waving tickets. "Look what I've got! For Yehudi Menuhin this Friday! Want to come? David gave me two complimentaries."

"Well, I don't know much about music.'

"Come on, it'll be great!"

"Where is it?"

"At Festival Hall, on The South Bank. How about meeting us there, at the bar? Come at 6:30, then we'll have lots of time before the performance."

The tube had a go-slow, so after being jostled in the crush with little hope of a train, I decided to walk. In and out the dark narrow lanes between row houses with brass door-knockers, steps up and steps down, I hurried with all the Londoners. Along the Embankment the strings of lights on the restaurant barges rocked to the rhythm of the river. Over the bridge The South Bank stretched in lights and reflection. Around my favourite landmark, the "Boy with a Dolphin," swam taxis and Bentleys on their way to the theatre. By the time I found the lounge, panting and apologizing, it was 7:45. Conrad was laughing with four other men, drinks in hand. As he called to me, one of them came forward. He was tall and bony with thick glasses and long black hair hanging in twists.

"Well, here's Maid Marian!"

"David, go easy."

"Why of course, the delicate handmaiden!"

Absurdly, I felt a small but mean barb of jealousy.

Conrad turned to me as he had on the first day, taking my arm. "Hi, Marian. Come and meet the others."

The chimes announced the performance and I settled into my seat beside him, with David on the other side. Out of the corner of my eye, I saw David pass him the programme and their fingers linger until they slipped lightly away. I hated David for being the one he touched. I sat scalded and confused in that plush seat while Mendelsohn's music sang all around me. The voice of Menuhin's violin called me to a place deep inside where I had never been. It was like a bird spiralling in flight through billowing clouds black, grey and white, then the gold and pink and mauve of sunset, back and back in time and forward in waves of limitless space. Grief and joy co-existed for all eternity. The applause broke the spell. That's when Conrad leaned over and touched my forearm. "Marian, here's my hanky. I think you liked it. Am I right?"

After the encore, David said, "We'll have to meet again, Marian. How about Sunday, for some real culture? We'll pick you up about one." Why couldn't I be smooth and adroit, like David?

On Sunday Conrad and David arrived in his "clapped-out mini" and we drove to the soccer match of the Spurs and the Wolves, I think they were. We screamed and swayed with the vast male singing and came away with ears thundering. Time for a pint. We walked to the nearest pub, crowded with Englishmen downing their bitters. David gave me sherry instead. I lost track of how many I was having. My mother had warned me never to be plied with booze, but that was all long ago, far away, and completely different. The shouting and laughing and singing became a blur, until I felt myself being bundled through the crowd and out into the dark slick street with brick doorways receding into the distance. I felt so sick I couldn't help retching into the gutter. I wanted to lie down somewhere and die. From the black angled shadows David's face had the illusion of a sneer. "Well, well, had a little too much, did we? Obviously a neophyte."

"Let's take her home, David."

Conrad stayed with me I don't know how long, sitting on the end of my bed, his face fading in and out of a fog.

"Marian, wake up. It's time to go to work. Your grandmother called last night from Inverness. She wants you to go up for Christmas. I said you were sick; you'd call her back. You are looking a bit green around the gills. How're you feeling?"

"Was I nuts? My head's killing me. Sorry for being such a twit."

"No, no. It was a bad scene, that's all. Here's a cuppa."
(In those days he knew how to look after me, I must say.)

Two weeks later, I boarded the train for Scotland. The English countryside, though the wildness was tamed out of it, was still a refreshing novelty from dusty old London. There was Grandma MacLean at the station. I would have recognized her even without the photos on our sideboard at home, she was so much like my father. She had freckles like me, but her white hair was well-trained, crimped in waves back to a roll at her neck.

"Och, here you are, Marian. Welcome. Now come along."

Briskly, we strode off to her house. We didn't linger in the street or garden, but proceeded up two flights of stairs to a tiny room under the eaves. I stood Dad's valise by the tiny high bed with blue satin coverlet.

"The lavatory is on the landing below. Now you'll take a cup of tea?" And she sat me in her parlour, on a polished wooden chair upholstered in floral petitpoint. "I've made a wee Dundee cake... shall you have a slice? Now you must tell me directly, how is your mother?"

She demanded to hear all the news: of Herring Cove, Vancouver, and finally about my life in London. All the details, and no shortcuts. She was unrelenting, and because I had such a sense of belonging to her, I suppose I let my guard down. I told her all about Conrad.

"Oh aye, you're smitten with him, lass. There's no turning back now. He sounds quite like your father when he was young. But keep your own mind, child. These magnetic young men, they're a caution. If he's half the boy your father was, he'll remain constant. Still waters run deep." (Meaning strong and silent, I suppose).

As we washed and dried her Crown Derby cups and saucers, she turned to stories of the past. Then she played the piano: "Drink to me Only with Thine Eyes," "Traumerei," the Chopin favourites. Settled by the fire, we leafed through her picture albums, and talked some more.

I learned about my dad's life as a boy. His ancesters were from the highlands, where story-telling was the way of passing on clan histories, as well as the news of the day. Stories kept the fears at bay: of illness in the fierce wet winters, and of rival clans, ready to swoop down out of the mist.

"He kept up the tradition, Grandma. When I was little, in all the places we explored around Herring Cove, he told me stories, about how things began."

"Is that so?"

"Yes, the forest and the ocean are full of mythical creatures. The native people explained this to him, and then he invented special stories, just for me."

"He did, did he? He was a fine lad. Do you have a tale to tell me, Marian?"

"Oh, there is one, Grandma...I think it might be about you too!" She leaned forward, eyes sharp – now what's this? I smiled inside.

"Well, you see... on the Western shore of our cove, there's a creek that tumbles down from the highest mountains where the glaciers are. It spills out onto our beach and slips away into the Pacific. Did you know that long, long ago, frogs lived in the deep ocean? They were bluish-grey then. One day Frog swam into the shallows, over the smooth speckled stones into the channel of our creek. She heard a voice calling her...so faintly that she couldn't hear the words. She was curious, so she swam upstream, following the faraway voice. The cedar branches leaned over the water, casting green reflections, flowing into Frog.

At last she approached the bank, and there in the sun sat grey Mouse Woman, sometimes called 'Woman of the Creek'. She was the oldest and wisest woman in the world."

Here I paused, to see what Grandma would think of this. "Go on, child. Go on."

"Well, Frog called in her high burbling voice, 'Woman of the Creek! What have you got to say to me?'

The dry and creaky words were scarcely audible. 'Come closer, come closer, Frog!' As Frog wriggled forward, her fins began to stretch, and she crept forward into the mud. Her tail split into two long legs and she climbed up beside Mouse Woman.

Frog was impatient. 'Now tell me! Tell me!'

Mouse Woman sat for a long time. Then slowly, in her dry aged voice she explained to Frog about the land: the mountains, dry plains, and forests, and how she was the granddaughter of Raven, who caused Light to come into the world. She told the long genealogy of the animals. Then Mouse Woman told Frog, 'Now you are transformed. You can move between water and land. Swim back into the creek. But visit me again. I have more to teach you.'

Frog couldn't resist the invitation. She was glad she didn't have to stay dry in the sun, so she swam away, but she wanted to hear more. So she came and went along the creek as the seasons changed, and so did her children, and their children. The Mouse Woman, in shifting forms, was always there to greet them."

We sat quietly for a moment, smiling at each other.

"Marian dear. Or shall I call you Little Frog? You have brought my son back to me, after all these years."

On New Year's Day she marched me back to the station, and hugged me swiftly. "Nay, you mustn't forget– he'll always be with us." And tears moistened her eyes.

"Thank you, Grandma." Wise woman mine.

On Monday morning as I crossed the square I saw Conrad on the steps of the hospital. "Conrad! Wait up! How was your holiday?"
He turned but said nothing. His face was rigid, like carved wood.
"Are you okay, Conrad? What's wrong?"
"I'm okay. How was your visit?
"No, you look terrible. Are you ill?"
"No." That's all he would say.
We plodded up the worn stone steps through the blackened brick passageway and on down the many-cornered halls, past the rows of photographed patrons staring down in black and white formality, to our treatment rooms, and the day began. Patients came for the slow building of their strength, or the slow retarding of their disabilities. Conrad worked with skilled hands, bending over and lifting patients in the usual way, but he looked like a weary soldier. At the end of the day, I suggested he come to my flat for supper. I was surprised at my boldness. He allowed me to lead him to the underground and up into the street again, along the cold windy passages of Earl's Court, around the hurrying crowds and lorries on the Old Brompton Road until we pushed open the peeling blue door to my place. We scuffed up the grooved stairs to the third storey, turned the big brass knob, wiped our feet on the worn mat, and at last sank down onto the wine-coloured sofa. He sat in a lump, staring in silence. What on earth had happened?

Ahead along the highway, the shadows are still long. A rhythm of fence stripes on the flat bleached ground numbers forward like a piano keyboard. The high-tension wires overhead are buzzing. The sharp corners of lonely silent buildings where no one talks to me are gone. I'm listening now, for a message. But so far, there's nothing but silence.

No sound of water rushing through banks of ferns leads me to an elder who will guide me.

No green canopy whispers over me while I crouch in an unfamiliar mind and wait to transform into someone who will survive.

No voices of my children playing in moist air remind me where I come from and where I belong.

Yearning though I am to pass through this barren place and leave it behind, it seems that for the time being it's my home and somehow it will have to be what sustains me. Yet there are no life-giving qualities in it that I can see: no food or water or place to hide, and most of all, no answers.

There is greyish brown ground... a horizon... and sky...that is all.

There is myself...this car...and shadows. Oh, and the sun. The angry dominant sun. All are dry.

Not quite. Inside me there is still moisture. In my mind there is still some green. I can live off that, for awhile. Green memory.

Conrad and I were meant to have a triumph here, the culmination of our professional excursion to China. We'd report back to America on our working partnership and how we drew our Chinese colleagues into Western Rehabilitation. We expected deafening applause. But no. It didn't work out that way. We weren't the partners we thought we'd been in England.

I've just realized why this seat is so uncomfortable. Conrad must have been the last one to drive, and it's all set up for his long legs. Little by little there'll be a shift in everything – to suit myself.

It was shocking to watch Conrad, slumped on my sofa in Earl's Court, composure and strength of purpose gone. I tentatively held his hand beside his knee. Stone-still, he finally exhaled in a deep sigh.
"It'll be okay, Con, it'll be okay."
Quietly he said, "I've lost my home."
"Oh, I'm so sorry. Would you like to stay here? There's a small room behind the kitchen. And Cecil will be leaving soon."
"Thank you, maybe for a while."
My flatmates didn't object. They hardly knew he was there, he was so quiet. Always washed the dishes, didn't linger in the bath, left early, went to bed early. Even when we all came in late from the pub, there was always a crack of light under his door. One evening I paused in the hall, watching him wash some clothes in the kitchen sink: scrubbing and wringing out, but so silent, alone and staring at nothing. It seemed he was in hibernation. We never talked about what happened at David's flat. I learned that where big feelings were concerned, he was a closed book. But it was miserable watching him, so low. I fretted about how to coax him back.
"Would you like to eat at Mario's on Friday?" no.
"What about a concert at Wigmore Hall?" no.
"Would you come to the party at Zerina's?" no.
"I have a headache." He'd sit in a dark corner of the front room holding his temples. There seemed to be nothing that I could do.
After work one freezing day in February, I had my head down against the wind on Shaftsbury Avenue, when a window display caught my eye: guitars, all colours, big prices, some not so big. The cheapest one was a ¾ size, but when the clerk played

it, it sounded okay, so I bought it. When I got home, he was sitting in the living room, on the window seat. "Conrad, look! This is for you!" And I pushed it into his lap.

At last he smiled but said, "It's good of you, but I don't play any more."

And he held up his hands: nails gone, cut down to nothing, moons cold and pale. I sank down on the couch. Then it came to me: he doesn't want this coaxing, this fluttering around. "What I meant is, could you teach me? Just chords and strumming, so I can learn some songs. Just a bit. I'd appreciate that so much."

For the first time in a long while, he smiled at me with his amber eyes. "Okay. Why not?" Standing up, he shrugged off his coat and folded it neatly on the window seat. Then he swung a side chair from the fireplace hearth and placed it in front of me.

"First you sit here, and put your left foot on this cushion. Rest the guitar against your left leg, above the knee. Now bring your fingers around the neck, drop your elbow, now angle your right arm so your hand is there. Here, let me turn your hand a little, flex your wrist and keep it still. The movement comes from your fingers and the elbow. Now try the resting stroke, like this."

And so we began. Each day after work, he worked on me till I could play the bones of a tune, keep the rhythm for a song, even manage some simple arpeggios. Our flatmates taught us some songs new to us. It kept the cold nights away.

At work and in the flat people got used to us being so much together. We must have looked a funny combination, Conrad tall and slender, me short and stocky. He was always so neatly put together, in co-ordinated colours, usually brownish pants and those patterned shirts he bought on Oxford Street, that went with his suede jacket. I still wore the tartan skirts and pastel blouses that my mother made, that never seemed to wear out, more often than not thrown on from a chair as I dashed after him out the door. (It was a bad habit of mine, hiding in bed, ignoring the morning lorries on their way from the market, that drown out the alarm clock and the click of heels in the hall.) My impossible hair, the variegated colour of beached logs, wouldn't stay out of my eyes in the wind approaching the tube. But his were the bronze curls around a Greek athlete's face. One morning, as we passed by the ticket wicket into the underground, I glimpsed our reflection – the tall and the small, so different but belonging together. That was one of those tiny joyful moments of feeling in exactly the right place.

We branched out to explore various parts of London. On Sundays we sauntered through Kew Gardens or Hyde Park, through Chelsea or past St. Paul's to the East End. Conrad carried food, so we wouldn't have to spend money. Thanks to my mother's camel coat, I was happy beside him in the bitter cold of February, leaning against the lions in Trafalgar Square, watching the pigeons bobbing for crumbs, and the double decker buses hurtling by. Sometimes we spent hours in companionable quiet. Other times we picked up our continuing conversations, slow and gentle like a cat pushing a ball of wool here and there, a quiet unravelling of our stories.

"You haven't mentioned yet, Mari, what brought you here."

"Vancouver felt pretty small. I guess I was bored, and maybe a little trapped. Quite a few of my friends were getting married after graduation. I just couldn't see that happening to me. "

"I know exactly what you mean... Did you always want to be a physio?"

"Since I was twelve, after my dad died. Where I come from, swimming is big. Our team coach was really great. One time when we went to Vancouver for a meet he took us to a pool where handicapped people received therapy. The therapists let us come in the pool and help with the children, playing water games. It seemed like the best job, to help people get stronger and be able to have so much fun again. I told my coach I'd rather do that than compete for a medal. After I graduated from rehab. school, there was no problem getting a job. Everywhere was so short of physios. English girls had their passages paid to come over. They said there were lots of jobs in the "old country" too. And it's where my parents are from. I guess I wanted to look up my roots. Did you come to London after graduating from McGill? Are you from Montreal?"

"No, I was born in Baddeck, in Cape Breton, but we moved around a lot. For most of high school, we were in Halifax. It was hard for my dad to find work. I suppose if I have roots, it's in Lunenburg, on the south shore. That's where my dad's from. He used to make Solomon Gundy, pickled herring, a bit like I brought for your lunch."

"Strong but good."

"Yeah. Keeping up the tradition. I worked at the VG in Halifax for a year. My supervisor told me I'd get super clinical experience over here."

"Why did you go into physio, Conrad?"

His face shifted into neutral, averted and outwardly calm. I was learning to catch this as a clue to feelings being submerged. "At first it was because of the miners. Black lungs, and broken-down backs. So many of my father's friends were crippled up. Like him...sitting around coughing. But it's a family thing, each generation going back for more. I was the youngest, and considered the bright one. So I got the chance to study, while the others were away working. I could listen to my mother play her fiddle, and read my books."

"Were you a bit lonely?"

Wrong question. He edged away. "No, just different."

I went back to a safer place. "There were fiddlers on the ship coming over. My cabinmate, Heidi, taught me how to polka. It was wild, mostly jumping and skipping and landing on each other's toes."

He laughed, watching me waving my arms around. "What about waltzes and tangos?"

"Sure, we had a go at whatever they gave us: jigs and reels, Viennese waltzes."

"Marian, if you like to dance, maybe we should try a few spots in London."

"Yes, let's! But where?"

"Oh, I know a few places in Soho we can afford."

It was magic. Conrad introduced me to another world, of old-time dance halls with cockney singers and smaller clubs clouded with smoke. Once when he was at the bar getting us a glass of wine, I thought: Marian MacLean, formerly of Herring Cove, now dancing in the heart of the world, with a wonderful elegant man. That was the first evening he kissed me. We took a long time to get started. Kids nowadays (or even then) would shake their heads in disbelief. But these things have to evolve. I knew Conrad needed a breathing space to get over whatever problem he'd had at David's flat. I trusted that he cared for me a lot, even though he couldn't express it. After all, he chose to be with me instead of someone else.

In March a letter from my mother described the blossoms on the streets at home, the bluebells at the side of the house, the chickadees perched on the back fence. The glamour of London looked bleak and man-made, joyless and sick. I considered using my carefully guarded money to fly home.

But Conrad and I hatched a better plan: camping in Europe. No one at work seemed surprised. Rosalba even offered encouragement. "Yes Miss MacLean, anyone can see you two are thick as thieves. A little heat is just what's needed. Spain, Portugal, the Riviera! How I wish you could pop me in that little backpack of yours. Now I have a small something for you. Look in the pouch at the back of my wheelchair. Do you like it? Yes, it's all little mirrors. It's from my country. The Kashmiri women are clever with their needles. Put it on. Toss the end over your shoulder. The green is perfect! It complements your eyes. Well it's a pleasure. Mr. Pereira looked all over London. I told him, she must have something to remember us by."

How could I forget this woman whose heart supported mine, and still does? She, as well as Grandma, and probably Sarah, knew all about what it means to love a man, but they had the grace to let me discover this for myself. Now, her body had betrayed her hopes, but she still projected her sense of fun to everyone. I had hopes too, and no thoughts of solitude.

At our farewell party the staff treated us as a couple, toasting our flight into the unknown. In the midst of the laughter and clinking glasses, an odd thought came to me: Conrad wasn't sorry to leave the Royal Memorial. Was I an excuse to move on? No, no. He really cared about me. He was almost mine now.

It's risky, setting off on a journey without instruction. At first you think there's only one road. But then you become aware of other trails branching off, and you're tempted to try those. Or scared to deviate, when maybe that obscure path would be the one that really gets you where you want to go. But I mustn't get lost now.

It wouldn't be the first time though. A very distant memory is of huddling by the escalator at Woodward's Department Store, wishing I could somehow be in our forest again with my dad. My mum must have brought me down to Vancouver on one of her expeditions for sewing supplies. I remember her and the store detective, he must have been, standing over me making soothing noises. She called me her little polliwog and gently scolded me for wandering off. Maybe I should find a phone and call her now. No, she'd only worry again. And set the kids on edge. There're all fine where they are. They think I'm still happy with Conrad. I must solve this mess before I rush back to them. I mustn't live for years with another sorrow, as I did with Josef. (The Angel: he's yet to come.)

Just where is the right path through this parched land? A phrase pops into my head: maps lead us, but where does silence lead? Along thin straight lines of smiles gone sour, to signposts that indicate where we have hesitated, and lost the direction we were headed in together. But when we were young our path was broad.

We set off, lugging our backpacks and the army tents that someone had given Conrad, through Victoria Station to the train, while the doors banged shut one by one, and we glided out past tenements and away to the sea. It was lucky we decided to rent the Renault, because France was freezing. The first night we couldn't face camping, with snow falling, so we walked around Paris. We climbed the Eiffel Tower, sat in Montmartre in a cafe to warm up, then finally found a place where the butchers go before starting work, and heated ourselves some more with onion soup. The Montreal days came in handy. Conrad had no trouble chatting with people in the street. They told us about the famous features of their city.

The next night we decided to pitch just one tent, and put both sleeping bags in together. That way we could conserve heat…so practical. In all our time living as flatmates, we'd kept the "proper distance" (as my mum would say). After our evenings of dancing in Soho, Conrad would kiss me, so lightly. And strangely (as everyone would say), that was enough, because I kind of filled in the gaps by dreaming about him. He was a fantastical prince. I hovered around him, waiting for him to heal from his mysterious sorrow at David's flat. We shared our work, and our guitar, so I guess we side-stepped the big issue of sharing ourselves.

But now here we were, in France with no work for our hands, and no other friends to distract us. Lying beside him in that tent changed me forever. I lay still as a cougar before it pounces, and breathed in rhythm with him. His slowed and became regular, and I had the luxury of listening to Conrad sleep, and I could smell his beauty. Very lightly, I reached out my left hand and laid it on his body in its down cocoon. It was a protective hand, maybe also a territorial hand. This first night together was my tentative beginning.

France was a backdrop for my personal drama. First I explored his hands. My fingers wandered over the guitar-string calluses on the pads of his left fingers, as we waited for our red wine, cheese and baguettes in village cafes. Then on to the curve of his nails. And the spaces between his tendons. Every part of him was like a delicious ingredient in a gourmet meal. I leaned over the table to be closer to his eyes, to look into his eyes so close that all I could see were the black centres surrounded by flecks and stripes of gold. When he played our guitar in the afternoons at a lay-by on the road, I would slip my hand onto his neck, and stroke it as he cocked his head slightly in concentration. He was perfect.

I even asked him how he felt about me. But he wouldn't say. Still, his smile was warm. He allowed himself to be lulled into pleasure. Little by little he responded to my hands, and at last we zipped our sleeping bags together. In our work as physiotherapists, our hands had understood many bodies; we weren't shy about this. But I wasn't prepared for the ecstasy. Neither of us could speak about it. His feelings as a man were a great mystery to me. They still are.

Nothing I saw in France during those weeks had the slightest significance for me. I was mesmerized by Conrad. The way our bodies leaved together was what fascinated me. We wove together, the little green frog and the elegant fleet deer. Driving through this desert now (with no stimulation or nourishment to speak of) is forcing me to look again at reality, at what's essential. Thinking back, I realize now that part of Conrad's power over me was his elusiveness. My hunger was much more than physical: it was for him to cherish me and meld in thought with me – to share everything, including the charm of France. But it wasn't like that.

Was it near Dijon? Yes, there were large fields on either side of the highway. We camped on the edge of a wood. I thought we were becoming a couple, but I hardly understood anything then, except what I felt myself. Taking for granted that he would respond with my intensity, I reached for him too insistently. He was so beautiful. It was like being in the mountains for the first time, with the purity of the snow above the tree line, and diamond-filled air. To be united with that, to move with that, was close to eternity. A silent place where no words ever existed.

But I couldn't divine what he thought or felt. That night his body was very still, hard and turned away, shutting me out. He told me silently with his body that he was somewhere else. Deep down I was rejected, but I didn't believe it. I made excuses: "Maybe he's shy of me." "He's tired." "He's cold." "I'm not perfect enough." It was necessary to be cautious and respectful of his privacy. My boldness shamed me.

My naïve animal self donned some new skins...was it called sophistication? It was certainly a protective cloak for my wounded heart. Having to endure me...was that a component in Conrad's brand of love? Strangers to each other still, we didn't possess each other at all. I decided that he was more complicated a person than I was, and it wasn't fair for me to push things too strongly. He was tentative about me and I must respect his reservations.

As Conrad drove through Southern France and on into Spain, I took to telling him stories; it was a way of passing the time.

"Conrad. Do you know about Dogfish Woman?"

"Should I? Who's she?"

"Now there's a tricky question. My father said she is very elusive. She swims alone and doesn't speak. She has an extra sense, that allows her to know without seeing. The legend says that she is female, but slips over into the male world. Then female and male share the same sense, but only for an instant. They glimpse each other in recognition. The other animals can't sense what she senses, so when we see her face, we don't know what she is thinking."

"You're a riddle-maker, Marian. What am I supposed to deduce from that?"

"Why, nothing...nothing."

By the time we'd reached Madrid, I had learned from him how to hold myself in reserve. I killed some of my enthusiasm for him in order to keep him, on some unnamed but powerful terms that only Conrad knew about.

I wish I could find a way to inhibit my desire right now, which is a plain and simple thirst for water in this desiccated land.

We spent the first afternoon basking in the Plaza Mayor, at last without winter coats. Or rather I sat, and Conrad walked around, watching the people and I watched him. Sometimes he would linger on the edge of a group of men, smoking and drinking coffee. At sunset we found a restaurant, had some delicious tapas and wine. About eleven o'clock, a flamenco guitarist came in, the waiter cleared a table in the centre of the room, and a singer began an entreaty deep in his throat. One of the customers, a blond woman in a black full-skirted dress and shoes with thick heels, was cheered and urged by her friends. She stepped on a chair and up on the table and began dancing. Everyone gathered around, clapping in a complex staggered rhythm, with hands spread like curved fans. They shouted or murmured "olé" to her. She beckoned to a friend to join her. They circled each other, glancing back, while the cantador wound a yearning spell around them. This was very far from English life, or Canadian, for that matter. Many people took their turn to dance. One man beckoned to me, others pushed me up, and I found myself in the middle of a pulsing, hypnotic circle. It was impossible not to follow the man fixing me with his black eyes. There was a sense of union and separation, submission and pride, cruelty and tenderness. This was the expression of the many forms of love. It was my initiation dance. Finally there was a cheering and they brought me back to Conrad. I was breathless and elated. "Wasn't that fabulous, Con?"

"You were great. You looked transformed. But give me Fernando Sor any day. Here, have some wine. One of David's friends told me not to miss the Prado. How about tomorrow?"

It was the first time he'd mentioned David since he had left his flat. "What's there?"

"Traditional paintings. I think it's an old palace."

"Okay, let's take a look."

We found our campsite by a miracle, in the dark. But as I crawled into our tent to prepare our sleeping bags, he called to me, "Oh Marian, I'll be back in a while. I'm just meeting some people at a cafe. Sleep well!"

But it was two a.m. Who were these people? Except for walking in the square today, he'd always been with me. A foolish suspicion lurked at the back of my mind: maybe I wasn't enough for him. But since my head was filled with the flamenco evening, I slept soundly as a stone on the hard ground.

Finding the Prado wasn't difficult. We joined the tourist flock walking down the grand avenue of the Spanish empire, now crowded with cars and buses. Passing between the Greek columns, we entered the first gallery, and were dwarfed by oil paintings in richly carved gold frames, of aristocrats, crucifixions, saints in stylized agony. We wandered dazed through room after room. And then a window opened on a terrible reality of the last century, of this century: "Los Fusilamientos del 3 Mayo en Madrid", by Francisco Goya. It was a painting of a man kneeling with legs apart, arms and hands spread, staring with defiant terrified eyes. His white shirt shone in the hard light directed at him in the bitter black night. Bloody bodies lay before him. Cowering figures, his comrades, huddled under his protection, but only for an instant, because from the right, faceless soldiers aimed their bayonet guns at him, in rank upon rank. I dimly sensed Conrad pulling me on, to the next room. These walls held only black paintings. I sank onto a cushioned bench. Here was Colossus with fist raised, his vast muscular body striding away from a chaotic horde of fleeing people and animals sunk into devastating darkness. And here, "The Witches' Sabbath," a ghoulish arc of gaping faces watching a black cloaked form, horned like a goat, poised for what? A sacrifice? The faces were brutish, curious, gloating, anticipating a black ceremony with relish. Faces, somehow familiar, loomed from the shadows. Royal vestments and glazed beauty were gone. But the worst image of all was a crazed naked man, Saturn, fiercely clutching and chewing on a headless child. His bulging eyes screamed his perception of his horror at himself: devouring what he loves. Devouring what he created. Devouring his life. Relentlessly, like time.

All language left my mind. I looked at what Goya forced me to see. This was as real as the pleasant rituals that decorated my days. This was the reality of the patients in ICU. This was what our society tried to cloak. This was a reality in me.

"Mari. Come outside. Come into the sun."

I found myself sitting on a warm stone bench with a trellis of pink flowers all around me. Conrad was sitting with me, holding my hand, with his arm around me. We stayed there, quiet, for a long time. Finally he began to chat to me. "Maybe we should head farther south tomorrow, how about Portugal, or we could see Sevilla or the Alhambra. That's a beautiful palace of the Moors, and in springtime they say it's very special, with orange blossoms and warm winds from Africa. Are you okay, now, Mari? Look, I've been thinking about something. I don't know what you'll think. Maybe we should think about getting married. Maybe we should just let it sit there as an idea."

What was happening to me? The world seemed bigger than my heart could contain. I was hanging between the extremes of sorrow and happiness.

"It's just a thought, Mari. We can talk about it later."

Sometimes I am living what seems to be a dream, and sometimes my thoughts seem more real and powerful than what I am living. I wandered with him around southern Spain and into Portugal. We walked through a misty deserted town, soft and grey as the pigeons at our feet. A path opened upward through a forest thick with flowering broad-leafed trees and black thin evergreens. A sweet perfume called us on. What seemed an enchanted building rose up ahead, its columns spiralling in black and yellow ribbons. White gardenias floated in the green. We sat down under a smooth-barked tree and Conrad pulled out our guitar.

He told me he'd play a famous piece by Tarrega, "Recuerdos del Alhambra." Rippling notes fell from his fingers and drifted away. They made a message that he would never say in words. They whispered about the sweetness of loving, and the yearning of hearts never full with the presence of their beloved, always far away in the eastern sunrise or the western sunset. The melody made shadowed arabesques of the patterns of sorrow for what could have been, or what might be lost. It spoke of a love that died in the last sobbing note. Could it be? That our love was so fragile?

He slung our guitar on his shoulder and we climbed the steps to that unnamed house. We watched ourselves in silver mirrors, and stepped on carpets soft as moss. Tables were inlaid with scrolls of ivory, where Cupid and Diana and fish dappled with jewels sat in frozen elegance. Open French doors led to a terrace, where we could watch white peacocks below on the lawn. Like brides, they nodded their tiaras this way and that, and swished their embroidered trains. I followed the curls of the railing with my finger, over and over tracing the pattern.

"Con, is something happening to us?"

"It's hard for me to talk about."

My words were slow as water dripping from a leaf. "Con. We can't seem to talk about it...our love. It's still so new for me. Remember what you said? About getting married? I wonder if you were just feeling sorry for me. I don't quite feel like a wife.

But I want to be with you forever. Sometimes I'm not sure if you feel that way."

"Marian, maybe you already know, but…" (This ominous pause. This long empty space.)

"What is it, Con?"

"It's just that…" (Please say it, Con. Whatever it is.) "I'm pulled both ways. I don't know if I can stay true to you."

A sharp fear, a truth, grabbed at my heart. "Do you mean you loved David more than you can love me?"

"Marian, I don't mean to say…"

I clutched the railing until it made grooves in my hands. How stupid could I be? Clues were staring at me all the time. Conrad was my lover in a fantasy. No. My love was real all right. I turned to face him, maybe to confront him in anger. But I stared at the devastation in his face. He wanted to be with me, but he had to remain honest with himself. How long had he hidden his true nature from himself, his family, his world? I couldn't look at him any more. I still wanted so much for him to be mine.

I gripped harder and said what I had to say, "Conrad. I want you to have what you need. It's not wrong for you to love a man, Con. It doesn't feel wrong, to really love what you desire."

He laid his hands over mine on the railing and we stood there, looking like a real couple at the balcony. A black ache spread through me. How could we ever find a way to be happy now, to be content in the world? Conrad might find it, but in a world that I would never know.

This road is ticking away the hours of where I've been, and where is that? Weary time on and on. Where Conrad is now I'll never know. I journey on, never released from my history and my obsession with myself. For the problem seems unsolvable: find-

ing contentment. He left me behind. This emptiness: will it be forever? Will I never find the end of this road?

I cannot go any farther... my eyes... closing. I'm falling by the side of the road, sleeping in the car, falling asleep inside. I hide, and seek for someone else, an alternate identity to inhabit. Fatigue takes over. I am slipping away, at last released from my waking mind that preys on, chews on, devours the happy self inside me cell by cell. At last I can drift on the tide of my unconscious and no one will interfere.

What a relief to have no dependent or tutor or leader to follow, or anything beyond this place on this road. Not even Conrad.

Only me. Lying in the still air.

Quiet voices from the distant past are no longer muffled. At last they have a voice, made from the heat and the sand. No conventions of thought are necessary. Only pulses of cells giving voice to each other, giving birth to each other in good order.

It's enough just to listen.

Retracing our steps back to London, all that time ago, was a conversion away from our romance. We took turns driving across the plains, over the Pyrenees, through the fields of France, still camping. Every day I had to be with him, but not like before. Waking up in my own tent, my hands would be sobbing, not the outsides that were facing the world, strung with workmanlike cables and girders. It was the soft insides, the palms and finger pads, the holding and stroking parts that were weeping: the cushioning, blanketing, private silky parts that wanted his beautiful head between them. The space between my hands was gaping potential. It knew the shape, it knew the texture, but it couldn't know the weight; my useless hands with their wasted framing and cladding couldn't enclose him any more. I pressed them together, to squash the feeling of his head, but they were tricky: the feeling concentrated and burned. I pushed them against my thighs but they tingled, they told each other what they could do together; they kept up that torturing current. So I made them open the tent and took them outside, plunged them into the campsite sink full of cold water, made them unpack and pack, pull up tent pegs, tie elaborate knots in fly ropes. I wanted to punish them, force them to replace every stone in those rock walls between the camp and the farmer's field. Flocks of crows flying over cawed at me in derision. And he just sat there on a rock reading his book: a classical sculpture left over from the Medici days, when gods and goddesses lived in the gardens of the wealthy. My eyes were burnt; I couldn't look at him. How can he do this to me? Be here day after day? I couldn't make myself small enough to hide from myself.

He drove, silent, while I stared at the fields of mustard yellow, poppy red, earth brown, grass green. Numbness set in. He rolled me like a rock from place to place. I was the millstone round his neck.

One evening, we were sitting in some cafe, somewhere. He stopped my hand as I was reaching for my wine glass, and said very quietly, "Mari, talk to me."

His eyes betrayed what I realize now was desolation and sympathy, but then I only wanted his eyes for myself. Still, his look pierced through my fog. I was able to look at him again.

"Mari, if only it could be different. You know I've wanted that more than anything. Please understand me."

I should have realized what it cost him to say that. His love didn't die on the balcony in Sintra. But then, I was wrapped up in my own crisis. I thought, out of my need for him: maybe I could do all the loving, and he could just pretend. That wouldn't be so hard for him, would it? No good. Say goodbye to romance, you silly girl. Get busy, do something useful.

Instead of my talking to him, I got him to talk to me. He loved doing research. He ferreted out every detail of the places we passed through. He explained how the poor and princesses alike were flung into the dungeons of the medieval castles. The iron clanged shut on the moaning darkness. I could relate to that: trapped forever, longing for what's outside. Drowning in the moat would have been better. He studied the maps and steered us through European culture. There were some windows by Chagall in Metz. So we hunted through the huge cathedral, to the shivery ringing of people reciting responses from some dark recess up into the vaulted air like spirits of the dead. Passing around some great columns, I saw shafts of pure colours striking the stone wall. Red, yellow, green, blue. Beaming from the stained glass of Chagall's vision of love: flying figures, and doves, and hope for our world. I stood in the beams of love. Conrad stood thoughtfully, sizing it up from various angles. We converted what had been real into something aesthetic. By the time we'd dropped off the Renault in Paris, I'd learned the lessons of his Finishing School, and had buried the tumult into something quite civilized. At a price, of course. No, that's not fair. Let's just say we adjusted.

The Channel crossing was rainy: grey sea and grey sky. Victoria Station received our train on time and the posted numbers clicked over that tiny detail. The hundreds of passengers, all intent on their own journeys, wove their path between each others' footsteps. Lines of people and bags, newspapers and dragging suitcases, followed and avoided each other. The women's lav housed the same bag lady as before, her brown wrinkled hands sorting and plucking her crumpled possessions while her grey hair wandered in wisps below the hand dryer.

Shrug on the backpack and away we go. Dodge the taxis. Pick up the pace. Run down the passage steps and into the tube. The men were like pasty mice in their tired grey suits, the women like owls with their black eyeliner that matched their black shiny boots. The heat of Spain had bled away by the time we reached our flat.

How about a cup of tea? We caught up on the news with our flatmates, and Conrad mentioned his plans to us all at once: he'd stay in London and specialize in respiratory work at the Brompton. I thought to myself: it looks as if he doesn't need me anymore. For anything. So I'll slot my dream of being with him neatly away, and hammer it shut. I wrote to my mother, "I'm coming home," and she sent me the money for a ticket. I was all set.

We took a last walk together in Kew Gardens the Saturday before my flight. Spring had hit London. We sauntered through the rhododendron groves, the huge oval leaves casting black shadows where the blossoms emerged, frilly and pale or in clusters of dark pink sheltering the nodding stamens. Passing through the bands of sunlit grass and shade, we walked in our customary silence. We wandered into a tea garden and found a table under a trellis of vines.

We chatted of ordinary things. "I'm going to give it another year, at least. The department at the Brompton has some good people. Lots to learn. And interesting cases. They bring them from all over. When I get back, I think I could start up a good programme in Halifax."

"Yeah, for sure."

"Thanks for your quilt and pillow. It'll see me through the winter."

"Oh, it's nothing. Would you mind keeping an eye on Sarah? Things aren't going so well with her guy."

"Okay, no problem."

I couldn't get the words out, about how I felt, finally leaving him. Even though we could never get married (that was far behind us now), the longing to be with him was still there. So I just said, "Conrad, I really hope we don't lose touch."

His amber eyes held mine for a long moment. He took both my hands and held them tight.

"You know how I'll miss you, Mari. I couldn't have another friend like you. If you ever need anything from me, I hope you'll ask. "

(All I want is you. But I can't mess things up with my emotions.)

"Oh. Thank you, Con." That's all.

What else can you say at a moment like that? I looked for some hint in him, of the bleakness in me. But he sat very still, draped in the garden chair on a patio edged by twining leaves. Whatever he felt then, it would always be his secret.

So I flew back to Canada, into my own land where I belonged. I wanted to get back to a place where I could walk around and recognize places, and neighbours. I was tired of Europe: of history and elegance and gardens with peacocks. I wanted a place that didn't have echoes of Conrad. Above all, no reminders of him.

I wanted to drive by a long lakeshore edged by a spiky line of mountain evergreens. I wanted to watch the creases of foothills rise to the bulky hips of a sheared-off peak half in shadow. I wanted to see snow wedged in crevices impossible for people to navigate, that flowed away in milky green between stands of tough trees going on and on. I wanted to be with trains that meant business: oil cars, coal cars, cattle cars in their dozens and dozens strung between blunt-nosed orange engines that growled in the tunnels and kept going for thousands and thousands of miles. I wanted to sit by a pond in the rain with the pungency of cedar trees dripping down, or by the ocean with grey sand and oyster shells. I wanted to come back West bit by bit, to shed what Europe did to me.

My ticket was for Edmonton; that way I'd get to see my old friend Barb from high school for a few days. Then she'd drive me to catch the early bus for Vancouver. There wasn't much to say at that ungodly hour. The streets were clear and the sky a pale goldy white. Through somebody's back yard trees there was a flash of startling red. By the playing field we saw the red eye of the sun peering under its long heavy grey eyelid over the line of prairie. By the time we headed down the main street with lights obediently turning green, it had woken up and was shining properly, with rays and shadows on the ground. We pulled to a stop and I hugged good old Barb.

"Thanks a million."

"Any time."

"See you."

"Bye!" I waved to the dog in the back window and pushed through the glass doors of the Greyhound Station.

Not much action here, no bustle. Just the early morning smokers coughing on the bench facing the storage lockers. I stare into a cup of coffee until I hear, "First call for Vancouver, stopping in Edson, changing buses in Jasper for points west."

I follow a Yul Brynner look-alike with a gold earring and phlegmy cough and grab an *Edmonton Journal* on the way. The herd of satchels, boxes for Greyhound Freight, tartan suitcases, duffel bags sit waiting to be stowed in their corral. I find an empty window seat past some other singles already dozing, trying to forget they're not still in their beds. I watch the driver shifting baggage. A stocky woman comes up carrying a beaten-up commode chair and gives it to the driver. Behind her a younger woman with long black hair swinging side to side pushes an aluminum walking frame in the lurching cross-over gait of the cerebral-palsied. At last the women, probably mother and daughter, are settled.

We're rolling to the outskirts: "Pegasus Stables," "The Black Dirt Co.," "Spruce Grove," cattle grazing with their calves, ribbed plowed fields. There's a flag stop at the Esso station at Entwisle. Guys in plaid shirts, jeans and cowboy boots worn down at the heels are standing around passing the time of day, and a lady with silver hair gets on with a small blue leatherette bag. Her slow and careful walk brings her to my seat and she tucks herself in. Her blue eyes in her brown creased face give me a quick greeting.

"Morning."

I'm intrigued by her. "Hello, how are you?"

"I'm goin' to a brand, near Kamloops. The 3-Y Ranch. You heard of it?"

"No. I haven't."

"My son's working' there. He's 49. 300 head are being branded."

"Are you going to work?"

"No, just watch. My son's not the owner. An old guy, 85 years old, he owns it. It's a ways out. There's a sign on the road." And she signals with twisted hand.

"Up in the hills? How many acres?"

"Oh, I don't know. Plenty. He's my second youngest. I got five kids. I lost one."

"Oh, that must be hard."

She shakes her white head, her array of bobby pins glinting. "Very hard. When it first happened, I didn't know what to do. There was no telling why."

"Yeah. I've lost someone too."

I feel her crinkly eyes on me. "You got to move on. Just move on."

A wise woman. Like Rosalba and Grandma. And the Creek Woman.

We leaf through the *Journal*. "That Trudeau – he's makin' a big splash. Pretty girl he's marrying."

"Kind of a flower child."

"Lots of those down at the coast. Where you from?"

"Vancouver. I'm coming home."

"Oh, that's nice. I got a brother in New West. But I don't go down much. Too much to do on the farm. My daughter mostly runs it now."

"Have you got grandchildren?"

We chatted on, about the kids, the land along the road owned by her relatives, about the winter just past.

"See? Those trees? That's from the fire went through a few weeks ago. Didn't get enough snow this winter. It's getting awful dry." The sun was low in the sky when she said, "Well, this is Kamloops."

"Have a great visit with your son!"

"Thanks. And you have a good trip. It's been nice talkin' to ya."

The driver helped her down the steps. Then I noticed one of her bobby pins was still on the seat. So I put it in my pocket for a talisman. She gave me a home-coming, planted me back on the ground. Canadians can survive a lot.

I dozed the rest of the way. It seemed to be kind of a milk run: (Hope, Chilliwack, Abbotsford, New Westminster) that finally nosed into the depot about 10:30. My mum was at the station. She even called a taxi, a big extravagance for her, to take her long-lost daughter through the familiar streets glistening with rain. Past Holy Rosary, over Burrard Bridge, along Kits

Beach with the bulk of Stanley Park across the water lying like a sleeping bear, past the tiny park with the stream, and then our street, where the tricycles were still parked in a heap in front of our neighbour's hedge. There were blueberry muffins on the kitchen table, and Mum's delphiniums in the water jug. What a relief, to have finally made it back home.

PART TWO

CORRESPONDENCE

10:30 Thursday,
The Sombrero Motel

Dear Conrad,

    I didn't sleep too badly, considering the trucks gearing up and down through the intersection all night. This motel is a far cry from the Oasis Resort, but it's more my scale. It was hard to get going again though, to crawl out of that no man's land. Around the back I followed a faint path that skirts the gas station and winds through old tanks, sheds and pieces of broken concrete. It stops just before the direction sign to the highway in front of a sign, "Eats". So that's what I'm doing. Scrambled eggs and hash browns and teabag dunked in a mug. Framed snake skins and cattle horns around the walls. Outside a brilliant blue little bird darting inside a spindly bush. At least it's quiet! I guess the truckers are miles out into the desert by now.

    It's weird to be writing to you when I doubt I'll ever see you again. Somehow I have to pin down what's happened: why did you have to leave me in the desert? We got on so well in China, even after all the years that we'd been away from each other. Let's face it: we've changed, should change, because of living. Like the earth, we've been worn away and shaped, both highs and lows. Physio practice has gone differently for both of us – the advantages of technology and team procedures, etc. are so much more important to you than to me. I guess I've been scrabbling with the kids down in the mud for so long. Crawling and sucking and cuddling and pooping have been such a big part of my life, and that must be pretty disgusting to someone as refined as you. You've still got it, though, why you went into this game in the first place: those poor old coalminers and your dad and all, and your mum's sweetness, teaching you the rewards of kindness. I mean the satisfaction of looking into a patient's face and knowing you've eased his pain, maybe even strengthened his confidence enough to give him a glimpse anyway, of a happy moment, or a bit of peace. We've just chosen or been channelled down divergent paths to the same thing. But you are still so much a puzzle to me.

What's it like for you to love only men? Not kind love or fun love but the wanting love: that's the mystery of you. Before, in Europe, it was odd how I could be so besotted with you. Well, no, it was natural. Though I hardly dared to imagine in those days, I was so conditioned. I can't believe how used I was to asking permission to even think! I still believed that the wrath of God would strike me if I listened to my body and my heart instead of admonitions about how girls should be. But you taught me how to listen.

When I realized that you didn't think of me like that, it was so puzzling: to imagine that you would feel that way about another man. That pain of wanting and not having. But are we really so different?

Speaking of wanting: something that we could have had but didn't, was children. Now there's a desire fulfilled, for sure. My exquisite children: touching them with my eyes and nose and lips, I tried to be as soft as a butterfly's wing, not to bruise even a cell of their delicate skin. At the same time, I imagined myself an enormous female colossus that could crush or repel anything that would think of harming my babies. There's no hint of that kind of love in the way I felt for you. But come to think of it, maybe there was. I often wanted to give your head a soft resting place, or tuck you up in a quiet corner away from harm. Isn't that weird to imagine little Marian with such possessive inclinations for such a magnificent creature as you?

So what was it you felt for me then? When we danced together in the tango I had the illusion that it was an awakening for us both. Maybe its elegance was the seduction for you: hanging on the pause before the next footstep forward, the quick reverse of the head, and both suspended in the music. That memory is still untarnished at least.

We've shifted, or perhaps solidified, in what we're all about: you into refinement and me into earthiness. It showed at the health conference: most of the delegates at that conference were like you, managing to polish the embarrassing bits of life away. Imagine our old patients: incontinent, speechless, one-sided, washed-up. Do you know how they feel, or is your focus now on your cleverness and technology?

It's all too sophisticated and I'm fed up to the teeth. It's because I've seen the ghouls, the same ones that Goya saw, in the mirror. I know what it's like to have disgusting cancer, to know that my self will be rotting, as sure as there's a tomorrow. So will you, despite your veneer of confidence. The anger toward my doctors I realize was a "shoot the messenger" syndrome. My pride at being one of them, part of the cool health delivery system, was shattered. And you're still on that side of the fence: calculating, analyzing, designing treatment programs, protected from the ugliness inside you – or so you think. You're cozy with your sauve colleagues, forming your pretty mouths around multi-syllables passed down from Hippocrates, thinking you're right about everything. It's "them" or "us" and now I'm part of them.

Do you think I didn't notice your discreet sneer at my confusion about what to eat at the conference? Even though in your view I should have recovered and "moved on" from my illness, you don't yet know about the deep, deep fear of making a false move and ending up fodder for worms, quite soon, not later. Will my collection of cells receive this coffee, butter, white bread and non-organic oranges as good food and behave themselves nicely and reproduce according to plan, or will they gobble it up and have a party? A wild, psychedelic, mind-blowing, cancerous party that sends us all tumbling down. You're part of the team that says, "Don't be a foolish child" and pats me on the shoulder and says, "Studies have not proved there is any connection between so-and-so and cancer; eat anything you like, in moderation of course." You must be joking. How come I've got cancer and you don't? What little secret are you really not telling me? Why do I meekly have to listen and humbly thank you and take my feelings to another professional? Forget it!

Conrad, the faintest whiff from you of that kind of smugness makes me hate you. You're betraying me if you don't support who I am now. If you say the slightest thing against what I'm choosing (like your comment at breakfast, "Honestly, Marian, do you need quite so much fruit; you're denuding the table, ha ha"), then you're the enemy. I'm mothering myself now; I'm trying to figure how to keep myself alive for a while longer.

But there's something else: I'll always adore you, in spite of whoever else comes along. You are my first sweet love, and you are almost as important to me as myself. If I could talk to you in person, hash it out: explain to you and you explain to me, maybe we'd have a chance. But no, I'm not permitted to mess things up. And so you're gone.

I embarrassed you; you need everything to be perfect, to protect you from the greasy disgusting stuff that threatens what you've created. The little kid inside you is well sealed up, but that's who loves me. You won't let him near me now. I've blown it, as far as your system goes. But you've blown it too. You've given up on me as a person. You left me in the desert. It wasn't a vote of trust that I can survive alone, oh no! It was indifference. Your silence said, "Our times in London, our times in China, our caring words for all the years in between, so what? You're really not interesting enough to be worth my patience and forbearance in this rather awkward time you're having. I may be back, and if so, you'll be around if I should choose to call." Oh, really? Little Maid Marian, is that it? Sorry, but I've moved on too.

I'm still here, and I'll find my way without your assistance. I haven't killed myself, by cancer I mean, and I won't succumb to being tossed aside by you. You can't fold me up. Absolutely and utterly not. I'll have to remind myself about this resolve; for sure I'll sink temporarily as I always have. But I can resurface; no doubt at all.

I guess I've cornered this booth long enough. The waitress is hovering around. She brings me the bill; her black hair is done up in a big silver butterfly clip. Her name tag says, "Soledad." She flashes me an unexpected, beautiful smile. She understands this kind of thing. "Gracias, Soledad."

Your former colleague,
Marian

In the years after I settled back in Canada, I saved all our letters, mine with carbon paper. Quite a lot went moldy when our basement flooded, though some I've carried with me all the way to China and back. I was going to show them to Conrad but somehow the right occasion never happened. Here's my envelope of old letters, from the bottom of my backpack.

Vancouver, B.C.,
May 19, 1969.

Hi, Con!

Thank you for your "welcome home" postcard–such a moment of nostalgia seeing old Nelson's Column, and thinking of us there on New Year's Eve, absolutely freezing. I have it on my bedroom wall, next to the one of us in Lisbon. The tennis club sounds great. I didn't know you played.

Mum said she liked the earrings from Toledo, though I don't know if she'll wear them. They look different in Vancouver somehow. She's well, but seems older.

Anyway, here's what I've been up to. A friend told me about a job at Workman's Compensation Rehab.: both acute and chronic injuries. I thought I'd better take it before I used up my tiny savings from England. Stopping in Edmonton turned out to be quite expensive, but it was worth it. Round my mum's neighbourhood everything's blooming and I've been planting her sunflowers and tomatoes. It's a lot quieter here: I guess I'll get used to it.

I took a trip with the West Side Hiking Club on the weekend. I thought I was in good hands but what do you know, we got lost. There were still patches of snow in the meadows, and the lake, the Mamquam, was still frozen. Eventually we found our way back by following a stream. They were a fun group so I'll probably go with them again. I hope your move to the Brompton will turn out well – let me know the details. And don't forget to give my love to all at the flat, and Sarah.

With love,
Marian

P.S: On the way to the bus stop after shopping with Mum on Hastings yesterday, something in the window of a china shop caught my eye. It was an old-fashioned tea set. Remember Sarah's aunt had us over that Sunday and served us with cups and plates of red roses edged in gold? It was like stepping back into that room with you. I could see the way you sat with your head tilted a little, patient with us ladies, submitting to being fussed over. This happens sometimes– then I remember that I can't have tea, or anything, with you any more.

love, M

The Flat,
August 4, 1969

Dear Mari,

    Glad to hear you're settling in. You can't imagine how hot it is in London. All the windows in the hospital are open, and fans going. The pneumonias, of course, are way down, so we occasionally relax by the fountain in the afternoon. I dip into some hazelnut yogurt, for old time's sake. Now that we're gone, it's just not the same at the old Royal, Sarah tells me. I must admit, the shine has gone out of the places where we walked together.

    I've been working with an excellent head physio. We're developing a programme with the surgeons to begin treatment right away in the recovery room, as we're hoping to prevent some post-surgical complications. There are still some old TB patients, with one lung removed or collapsed. The asthma and bronchitis service is the biggest though, and important for me to learn for the future.

    Enough about me. Thanks for your letter with your new address. Yes, it's probably a bit late to be living at home. Your roommate sounds fairly compatible. I've been thinking of leaving the flat (everyone sends their love by the way), because I've met some guys at the tennis club who are renting a house, further out, quite near Kew. It's on the Piccadilly Line so the commute won't be bad at all. It's not final so I'll send the address later. I ran into some of David's guitar friends, who invited me to the summer festival in Bath. Some bright new sparks are playing, and I hope, Bream.

    There's the doorbell—we're off to the pub. Keep having fun.

                              Love from the "Old Country,"
                                                  Con

October 23, 1969

Dear Con,

How are you doing? Sorry it's taken me so long to write. I've been quite busy.

I've got to tell you about a man I've met: Josef. Actually he was my patient at WCB. Came in for an accident to his hand. He's a carpenter, builds lodges for helicopter skiing. It's very cold sometimes, even in the summer at the end of the construction season, and there was some snow. His saw slipped and sliced into his thumb. There was some nerve damage, so he's needed time and rehab. Fortunately it's not his dominant hand. He may get pretty good function again. He's dying to get back to work, unlike a lot of other guys at the Comp, the ones in tedious noisy work like driving the huge road-building machines.

He's not tall but made of muscle, has black hair and beard, and his eyes kind of twinkle out from the thicket. (Have you ever been tempted to grow a beard? I can't imagine it, somehow. It would hide your wonderful long mouth and the angle of your jaw.) Anyway, he sort of booms around: fills the doorway, you might say. Our relationship isn't what you'd call intellectual. In his culture it's okay to be chubby. In fact, he thinks I'm some kind of gorgeous. Can you believe it? (Don't laugh). He's taking me dancing, but it's not the tango, like we used to do. He's crazy about music from someone called Howlin' Wolf, and Leon Russell, a mean piano player. So I'm having a good time, to put it mildly!

Lots of love,
Mari

December 9, 1969

Dear Marian,

Hope you're enjoying your first winter at home for awhile. It's been bloody freezing over here. Thanks to your quilt, I'm surviving in my new abode with this stoical crowd of Englishmen who don't believe in using the puny heaters they do have.

I've been humming a song by Donovan lately…reminds me of you of course. It's something about "sun so high, yellow in the blue blue sky… many good times we have had, we've been happy, we've been sad…"

Work is rolling along. I presented a short paper to the Society of Physiotherapy meeting two weeks ago. Who should be there but old Phynn. At first she gave me her evil eye, but after my presentation she came up and treated me like a human being. Was asking after you and said to tell you Rosalba died. She remembered you two had something special, so maybe she's not such a thorough dragon after all. Miss Hedley has retired to her family estate in the Cotswolds. Phynn goes to visit her and they definitely have or have had something going together. Oh, she also said Sarah's getting married to one of the house doctors—guess she ditched that twit she was running around with when you were here.

Speaking of eligible men, are you sure you need to jump into this so soon? The last thing I want to do is mother you, but am just thinking of how easily you are swept off your feet. On the other hand, he may be just the right kind of fellow for you. I'd never laugh about what he thinks about you. I've always thought you have a unique kind of beauty. Don't ever change. I hope you're very happy with him. This makes it easier for me – the guilt. You were so innocent, it seemed important to protect you from myself.

Have a super Christmas. I'm spending the hols in Austria. Andrew, from the house, is introducing me to skiing. Should be amusing.

Fondest love,
Con

Reading this over now, I'm getting the hint that there was a deep affection there, that Conrad has a vulnerable heart after all. It's with a certain amount of chagrin that I realize how little I understood him, especially after becoming so involved with Josef. I guess I closed the book on thinking about who Conrad really was.

Everything that interested me seemed to delight Josef. So when our friendship reached a certain stage, it was natural to take him to my favourite place – Herring Cove. What we'd find was no longer certain, since my family was gone, my father dead, and the place itself now off the map. We took a long weekend at the end of November, and caught the water-taxi across to The Landing. Even after all those years, the cormorants were still hunched in a black row on the end of the wharf. One stood on the highest pylon fanning its wings like a bat. Then it skimmed out over the water, neck extended, and the others followed. The clouds in the west were piling up over the mountains, which were patched with snow on the clear-cuts.

Josef held my hand. "Hey Doll, what a big sigh...you okay?"

I laughed. "Come on Josef, let's see if the cabin's still here."

Shouldering our backpacks, we picked our way along the shore on the old boardwalk, now broken with gaps that we had to leap over. Salmonberry bushes with a few leaves still clinging on reached down from the cliff and cascades of rainwater dripped into the sandstone. The high tide had pushed up a thick fringe of jumbled seaweed all along the sea's edge. Detritus from the ocean: dead crabs, bark from the log booms, shell fragments from clams, mussels, oysters, tangled in the slippery green, orange, black and frailest pink weed. I led Josef through this squishy carpet to the base of the huge Douglas Fir, where the trail to our cabin used to be. It's the best eagle perch on our cove, because it's so tall and leaning outward toward the ocean, and the top has been blasted of branches by the wind, so there's room to land and sit up there with companions and watch the world with eagle eyes. Sure enough, two dark birds with white heads and yellow beaks hunched there, silent and still. "A good omen, Josef! It's still home!"

I could hardly wait to find our cabin. We pushed through the thick salal undergrowth, between the broad-leaved maples, their huge goldie-brown leaves tossed everywhere. Our boots sunk into the wet earth with a sucking sound. Josef wasn't used to this! His place was snowy rocky slopes. Eventually we emerged into a clearing, overgrown with brambles and alder saplings, and there was our cabin. You'd think that I would be shocked by how downtrodden it had become: the shingles lifting, windows broken, brambles creeping into the boards, but no…it was so recognizable as my family's life, like seeing your childhood in a glance. I ran around looking for traces: my mum's washtub overturned, the rope swing my dad made hanging with the log seat still hooked in the fork of the maple, axe and shovel and rowboat leaning against the back wall. Inside we had to set to work right away, sweeping away the mouse droppings and spider webs with cedar boughs. Josef found a coffee tin of nails and with a rusty axe head, nailed down the shingles. By nightfall we'd made a very satisfactory nest for ourselves. Josef made a firepit and we roasted a feast of potatoes and sausages and the last harvest corn.

In the night it poured with rain but we were warm in our cedar bough bed on the floor. It was so obvious that Josef belonged with me. You don't have to say much when you know that for sure. In the morning I tried to find the place where my dad showed me the Indian petroglyphs, but it had disappeared into the dripping green undergrowth.

While we waited for the water-taxi to pick us up at sunset, we sat on the wharf swinging our legs over the side. We had a spying contest, who could see the most sea creatures in the water. "Spider crab! Sunstar! Anenome! What's that? Mermaid! Ah c'mon Josef…play fair. No! It's your reflection…that counts! My God! What's that? It's a sea lion!" It slid along underneath us, and came up for air, blowing in a gusty snort, whiskers erect. It looked at us with glossy black eyes and then submerged in a snakey black curve. From out in the middle of the cove the whack of a flipper echoed against the cliff. "They're fishing, Josef. But it's not the herring season. I wonder why there're here."

"Babe, that is so awesome. They're spying on us…two happy humans, they're saying."

"So Josef – you like it here?"

"Don't you know, Little Mugs? I'd like it anywhere…I'm just orbiting around you." He held onto me like a great big bear. Totally mine.

April 26, 1970

Dear Con,

Thanks for your postcard from Spain in February. Josef says the Pyrenees have some good skiing. He pointed out on the map where you'd been. That's a bit further east than we got, isn't it? (I told him how much you meant to me in Europe and how we parted.)

Josef wondered at first about my writing all the time to you, couldn't believe I'd spend so much time on "just a friend." Now he calls you "Jack in a Box" because I keep all your letters in a box.

The wedding was small; Barb was my maid of honour. Two of Josef's climbing friends were best man and usher. Here's a photo outside the church. We had the reception at a hotel downtown, the Sylvia. My mum met Josef's parents and grandmother for the first time—they got on great. She showed them around Vancouver while we were away in the Bugaboos. It was fantastic! Far too crazy skiing for me. Maybe you could come out sometime. We're planning on building a place at a new ski hill called Whistler, if we can get some land fairly cheap.

Congratulations on being made assistant head. It's good that they recognize a gem when they see him. It's amazing how quickly you're climbing the ladder. Nothing exciting at work here. Except the girls gave me a lovely shower. Josef thought it was very quaint, all the hat-with-ribbons stuff and blindfold games. Anyway, they were very kind and we're pretty well set up.

His hand is almost completely restored so he has started work again for the summer. That means he's away quite a bit—there're some new lodges in the Kootenays starting up.

But that's okay; I can probably get some time off and stay up there with him.

Say hi to Kew Gardens for me.

Your dear friend,
Mari

December 12, 1970.

Dear Mari,

Thanks very much for the birthday present – delightful that you remembered. The moccasins are super warm and still have that good woodsmoke smell.

They gave a surprise party at the house—got me out before on some pretext. It was quite a bash: champagne and a groaning table of delectables. It was amusing observing the guitarists trying to relate to the tennis players: eventually they discovered something in common—Lloyd George was their father, as the song goes. The work people put on a rather hilarious skit. And then the musicians couldn't be held back. Several days of cleaning up the debris followed, and luckily all the neighbours came so we didn't have any repercussions.

I should tell you about a workshop I attended in October – just up your alley, I think. It was at the Western Cerebral Palsy Centre, started by a physio, Berta Bobath, and her husband. Very impressive theory and demonstrations of their approach toward neurology. One of the interesting aspects is the subtle communication and movement between therapist and patient, without words. It's an interplay of feeling and response on both sides. So you can do this with young infants, elderly aphasics, anybody. The gaps or damages in movement and balance are filled in by the physio, and gradually the patient takes over: that's the hope. She calls it an art as well as a science. I might be able to apply this to chest treatment, such as twisting and mobilizing the rib cage for greater lung expansion. Have you come across this in your travels?

Am thinking of moving on in the near future. Some people at the VG in Halifax want me to work with them on developing post-op care. I think I've almost learned enough for that.

Keep having fun! You're not letting this Josef of yours dominate your thoughts, are you? He sounds like an earthy fellow – presumably that hits the spot at this stage. Congratulations on finding the piece of land. Should be no problem throwing up a house as long as you do the sawing. Best of luck.

Yours, one year older,
Con

> We're proud to announce:
> It's a girl! Emily Anna
> Born on: March 7, 1972
> Weight: 8 lb. 11 oz

March 13, 1972.

Hi Con!

We did it! I was beginning to doubt we'd actually deliver this baby. It was horrendous, at one point I thought I was being split in half—but you don't want to know that stuff! Josef was completely involved: breathing, practising our song (Leon Russell's "Sweet Emily"), rubbing my back, mopping my brow, timing the contractions. I began to get quite hysterical, the contractions completely overwhelmed me, but Josef was able to calm me down. It's the first time I've ever been in a hospital for myself. It's quite a switch! When she came out, they gave her to Josef to hold. My mother said this was unheard of in her day. So now we are into breastfeeding. I won't bore you with the details, but it is consuming me 24 hours a day.

I adore her already. I'm exhausted. It was so wonderful when I nursed her on the delivery table. Her little mouth clamped on right away, and I held her tiny hand. She has some of my father's features, especially around the brow and nose. I can't describe it. I wish he was able to see her. My heart is so full. I wish you could come and see her too.

Love from
Mother Marian!

University Hospital
Halifax, Nova Scotia
March 26, 1972

Dear Mother Mari,

Congratulations! And to Josef! March 7 is a happy, happy day. I hope you'll be sending me photos at every stage, though I can't say I can see a resemblance just yet. It does all sound pretty grisly, but for a precious result.

Enclosed is a present from my mother. I was back to Cape Breton on the weekend and she was thrilled to hear your news. It's a baby shawl made by her grandmother, preserved quite perfectly, I think you'll agree. She's very fond of you, what with you pulling me through thick and thin in the London days. You're right good as far as she's concerned. And since she's not likely to have any progeny from me, she wanted you to have this, to think of your little girl as part of our family.

She has loads of other grandchildren now: my brothers and sisters are not losing time. She joined my eldest brother in some rollicking tunes after supper on Saturday. We stomped the floor boards young and old; my niece Stephany is quite a pert little dancer, hopping in her kilt. On Sunday I took my brother's horse for a ride to a favourite spot, the Margaree Valley.

My headaches have been acting up lately. A colleague from Dal gave me something else to try.

Did I mention that Andrew has decided to emigrate? I don't think it'll be difficult for him – he's an electrical wizard and Nova Scotia seems to need those at the moment. I have an eye on a small house near Dalhousie. So we're going to set up together. He doesn't seem to have the stage fright about it that I do. A bold Englishman, ready for the New World. Let's hope Halifax is ready for us!

The Neptune Theatre has had an excellent season, not comparable to London of course, but quite entertaining for the winter months.

Take good care of yourself, as well as your beautiful daughter. Keep me up to date when you have time!

With love,
Con

There wasn't a ceremony for him, marking that important milestone. There should have been. Would he at last be as happy as Josef and me?

January 3, 1973.

Dear Conrad,

Thank you very much for your Christmas card and cute teddy for baby Emily. I'm a bit late with my cards this year. Your house looks charming, and I'm so pleased to have a photo of Andrew at last, his nice face to place with his name.

Our house is almost finished. Josef had a big push on for the Christmas season. We hosted the ski patrol party this year. One Friday night we were at the coffee shop at the bottom of the gondola (they turn it into a cabaret some evenings) and Terry Jacks was there with his band. It was packed, a sweating mob. Anyway, you can't keep Josef down. He may be nimble as a spider on a rock face, but on the dance floor—watch out for your toes! Musicians love him: the joint's jumpin' in no time because nobody can resist my Josef. So at a break they were yakking away, and Josef persuaded them to come play at our party. So they did. We made piles of food. You can't imagine how these mountain people eat. People brought wonderful stuff too: strudels, kuchens, tortes.

Everyone loves the mountains so much! Josef and his friends hike beyond the last T-bar to a superb bowl on the other side of the peak. It would be great if you could see it. Why don't you bring Andrew out sometime?

Emily is running around now so we had to childproof our house. It's amazing what she gets into. She'll be a climber like her dad. We're expecting again! Wishing you a great 1973. Keep in touch!

Love as ever, Marian

August 25, 1973.

Dear Conrad,

    It's not often I get to send you a postcard! Josef spirited me away for a few days. We brought baby Hans of course (named after Josef's dad), and left Emily with my mum. I wanted to give him a second name, Hamish (after my father) but H.H. seemed a bit much, so we settled for my grandfather, Broderick. It's lovely here, having the chance to swim again—hot pools any time of the day or night, and walks by the lake. Wish you were here!

Love,
Marian

November 8, 1973.

Dear Marian,

Hope your brood is thriving, and the parcel arrived.

Have just returned from taking Mum to Lunenburg for my dad's funeral. The Zion Lutheran Church was filled with faces from the past, the children bearing an uncanny resemblance to my cousins when we were kids. We all walked down Fox Street to the reception at Oma's house. I nipped over to Zwicker's to get some candles, and felt like a ghost of my smaller self. Oma gave me a lantern, a pen knife and an old bible that had belonged to my dad. One has the illusion of being able to go back in time.

Andrew has booked us a long weekend in Toronto later in the month, ostensibly an early birthday celebration, but really a chance for Andrew to see Karen Kain and Frank Augustyn. He's nuts about the ballet.

Thought I'd look up some old colleagues from McGill who are now at the Wellesley. We've decided to establish an inter-provincial respiratory group. ICU techniques are becoming more precise now, streaks ahead of the dear old Royal.

Did you know that the Bobaths are giving workshops across the States, and they'll be in Seattle next summer? Since you're getting back into the fray, and so interested in kids, I thought you might not want to miss it. Enclosed is the brochure. Let me know what you think, if you go.

Andrew has a new contract with an aid project in the Caribbean. Lucky him.

Regards to Josef, Emily and Hans.

Fondest love, Con

Feb. 21, 1974

Dear Conrad,

    I was looking back through my box of letters the other day, and I find it hard to believe that it's only five years since I was sitting in Kew Gardens tea shop with you. Now I have two little kids and you have a flourishing career, etc.! We were such free agents then, no obligations to speak of. But I wouldn't trade it for now, would you? Sometimes I barely get my dressing gown off and clothes on before the day is over, there's so much to do with the kids. Emily is talking a blue streak, and very demanding, now that Hans is crawling after her toys. She can't get enough attention, especially when Josef is away working. When he's home, they have such a riotous time together. They love crawling all over him, and he pretends to be a bear or a wolf. The screaming you wouldn't believe. Or he gallops them around like a horse. He makes them wonderful toys: a wooden duck on wheels, a farm set, an old-fashioned top painted in circles of all colours. He's started on some little skis for Emily next winter.

    I've been offered a small physio job, to buy a few extras and keep my licensing up to date. The Whistler clinic needs relief people once in a while, especially during the ski season. It's been a while, but I'd like to give Orthopaedics a try. Have signed up for the Bobath course – thanks for the idea.

    We all send our love to you and Andrew.

                                                        Marian

January 27, 1975.

Dear Con,

What a delightful spot to spend the holidays! You and Andrew look like tanned gods. Imagine running into Paul McCartney! How I wish I could be in Barbados too!

I'm getting my feet wet in a different way. Josef has no job right now because it's just too cold for carpentry. So he's babysitting while I help at the clinic. It's quite a challenge. I have all my old rehab notes, and ortho texts at the ready. The patients are a far cry from the Royal though. They're all healthy, muscular, and raring to go. It's like treating race horses. As yet I haven't had much chance to practise the Bobath techniques, but am so glad you steered me onto it. The students were so keen, and from all over, (one from Tallahassee, with a wonderful speaking style). Because she stressed the healing-art aspect, everyone can exercise their own sensitivity toward the patient, and this is taken as legitimate practice. The unmeasurables, like what the therapist feels in her hands, such as quality of spasticity, is acknowledged. I'd say it's augmenting my ortho practice here, and even the way I handle my own kids.

They love having Josef around so much. I said any bad habits they have will be his, but it's more likely to be the other way around.

I bet you hated stepping off the plane into all that snow! We even heard about it out here! Must get to bed for an early start tomorrow.

Your dear friend,
Marian

June 11, 1975.

Dear Marian,

Thanks for your letter last month. You were asking how Andrew is getting on. Hopefully well, though he has been in Barbados since March 20, supposedly on a hydro project. It's also likely that he's been seduced by the sunny Caribbean lifestyle. Thanks for your invitation to visit you. I'm quite committed to what's going on here, but would certainly like Andrew to meet you. He's dead keen on seeing the real you after my glowing descriptions! I've even had occasion to wonder whether we should have followed through on my suggestion outside the Prado. We probably could have had a wonderful life together. Tricky looking back though, isn't it?

I have, however, more down to earth matters to occupy myself with now. The dean has been urging me to take at least a Master's degree in Health Administration. Dal doesn't have a programme yet so he suggested McGill. The hospital is being quite generous: one week off each month to visit my preceptor and three months next spring for concentrated study.

If you're finding Hans has persistent colds with protracted coughing, you might consider a lung function test (any respirologist can do it). In the meantime, take good care of yourself: don't let yourself get too haggard. Giving your all benefits others, but maybe not yourself.

By the way, a protégé of Julian Bream has landed in Halifax, so am enjoying some lessons after all these years.

Yours in memory,
Conrad

As I sit in the shadow of the open car door, I'm stunned by his words…his second thoughts. How could I ever have been his wife? What virtuosity of his heart would that have required? The blankness of sand stretching on is accented by black outcroppings of rock. Waves of air blur them and seem to throb in the same rhythm as my blood.

April 10, 1976

Hi Conrad,

The snow is still great! Are you tempted to come out? Your photos from Portugal took me back in a flash. I was touched that you wanted to show Andrew that magical place at Sintra.

You're obviously made for grad school, and I'm not surprised that you've been singled out by the Dean.

Hans, it turns out, has asthma. I could kick myself for not realising. It's not too bad if he can avoid colds and if I keep the house super-clean (what a hope). We can't bear to part with our dog, Shep, though.

All's fine here—very busy. Have taken up quilting. At last I have a use for all the scraps from making the kids' clothes. A friend from the preschool, Michelle, got me to go with her to the Pemberton Quilting Club. It's a different crowd from the Whistler folks: mostly farm women—so practical, but with this arts and crafts fever—I love them. They chat away the whole time: important stuff like kids and men and growing food. Michelle says I have a talent for picking colour. She says people with green eyes usually have it. Have you ever heard this? I'm learning the names of all these beautiful shades: Prussian blue, Alizarin crimson, Cadmium yellow, like in paintings. So I'm making you another quilt, to replace that London one – if you still have the tattered remains!

I dragged Michelle off to see Jose Greco in Vancouver! We had to stay overnight at my mum's. The guitarists were fantastic, riveting their eyes onto the dancers, especially one in a white dress edged in black who swished her train of ruffles this way and that. Michelle said, "Forget the quilts! We gotta make ruffles!"

Please pass my warmest hello to your mother.

Love,
Mari

He did come out for a bit of spring skiing, but the letters are silent on that subject. Andrew was away on a business trip. I guess I built it up into being a wonderful reunion, which it wasn't. From the first minute, Josef seemed very weird. Instead of his usual self, he went all stony and formal, and Emily was horrible. She threw Con's present, a beautiful china doll, over the balcony and smashed it, and refused to speak in anything except Rumanian (the few words she knew from her grandparents.) I thought things would calm down when we took Con up to the Back Bowl; it was the most glorious clear day. Unfortunately Josef decided to take us to the new powder on the West Bowl. I can't believe he was deliberately mean, but Con just wasn't used to the deep powder on such steep slopes, and he wiped out time and time again. At the lower part on the Gondola Run, the combination of ice and slush about did him in. I was furious. Josef herded us into the bar and virtually ignored us, carrying on with his buddies like they were going out of style. All that yahooing was the last straw for Conrad; talk about mortified.

We never said a word about it…that was the trouble. I tried to please him more (make nice dinners, drive him around, but nothing worked.) He became more and more polite. And then he withdrew back to the cultured East. Josef even had the cheek to joke about it on the way home from the airport. "Well, Doll – he couldn't cut the mustard, eh? Didn't go for my farewell Big Bear Hug?" Oh well, some things are best forgotten.

9 Sept./76

Dear Mari,

Just a quick note from a cafe on St. Denis.

Am itching to get started on this coming term. My advisor has just got back into town, so am meeting him this aft. Enclosed is a copy of our research findings in the current CPA journal.

Last night a McGill music student played a programme of Villa Lobos: very challenging rhythms and interesting harmonics. So am going to tackle that too.

By the way, was leafing through my sheet music looking for some Sor studies, and came across the pic of us at the farewell party from the Royal. Gave me a bit of a pang. You were wearing your green dress, the one for dancing the tango. Your hair was longer than I remembered, over your shoulders. Your eyes were extra-green, and you gave me quite a radiant smile. I can see why Josef fell for you. Funny where life takes us, isn't it?

Andrew's left holding the fort for a change. Keep well.

Love,
Con

20 August/1977

Dear Mari,

    Of course; I am honoured! It's a first time I've had a baby named after me. You are very kind to think of it. I have your photo of Emily and Hans, running through the sprinkler, on my desk at work.

    It's been quite hectic here. In June we had the stone-laying ceremony for the new N.S. Rehabilitation Centre. Exciting event really: Premier Regan, the Dal crowd, hospital people, loads of interested bystanders. It'll be a leap ahead in advocacy for the disabled, as well as top rehab.service. Now we're getting ready for the fall term. And the inevitable painting of the trim around our house. Andrew rewired it this spring so we can avoid having it go up in flames.

    Keep cool! With any luck when Josef returns from Blue River (wherever that is), baby Connie will be able to smile.

Fondest love,
Con

April 27, 1978

Dear Con,

Hoping things are fine with you. It's been ages since I've written. I seem to be in a whirlwind with the kids. Am helping at Hans' preschool, a co-op which we run ourselves. The mothers look after each others' babies as well; that makes it simpler with Connie. She's so much more easy-going than the others, chuckles away while we pack her here and there. No more tip-toeing around at nap time. Michelle, who's become quite a close friend, puts her youngest baby on the washing machine to sleep! So thunderstorms are a piece of cake.

Which reminds me, you think you know someone so well and then you don't. Josef, it turns out, is a cakemaker. For Emily's party he made an enchanted forest cake with fairies, mushrooms and flowers, and animals standing among some quite outlandish trees. Her 10 friends demolished it. The intense interest over the presents is quite something. And of course you have to pass out loot bags.

Have you been keeping up with this nuclear testing? It puts me in such a panic over our kids' future. And the population explosion, what a mess. The lifeboat analogy is too horrible to contemplate. And the poisoning of the Great Lakes, and chemicals being used on everything. There's so much to worry about.

Sorry to end on this gloomy note. I feel quite distracted lately, trying to keep all the balls in the air. Josef is taking a break, climbing with some old friends before the season starts again. Give our regards to Andrew; he's very lucky, to have you.

With love, Marian

May 3rd, 1978

Dear Conrad,

This is to tell you that Josef died in the mountains on Thursday. The RCMP phoned me early Friday morning. Two of his group were not injured so badly. They were able to get back with the news. He was roped with his climbing partner but they both fell. There was an avalanche and rock slide higher up. It was near Mt. Assiniboine in the Rockies.

At the service yesterday, his friend Orly gave the eulogy. He said he died doing what he loved to do. What about us, who he loved just as much?

I can't think what to do. I'll never stop waking up without the thought of him lying broken. They got his body out, and his climbing partner, so we had a proper funeral. His parents came over for it. People have been very good, especially with the children. Emily is taking it hard. She understands more than Hans and Connie.

I wanted you to know about this right away.

With love,
Marian

I thought it was the end. My life, gone. The world looked different after that day. The sun, however, insisted on rising and setting, grinding around the sky as usual.

This is a peculiar landscape. Nothing is recognizable. These so-called plants are like rag-tag bouquets of bent black wands, each one topped with glowing cigarette ends. The colour of huckleberries, but certainly not edible. I have to stop and look more carefully. No. Not anywhere near like real flowers. Not like that sympathy basket Conrad sent me. All white: lilies, orchids, baby's breath, even gardenias (he remembered about the gardenias). He knew just how to wrench my heart. There's no shade here whatsoever. If I angle the car toward the fence, maybe I can sit against the wheel and not get burnt up. That must be Mexico in the distance.

Now is the time for thinking about Josef, my crazy adorable angel. Our marriage was simple compared to my friendship with Conrad. Sometimes I chuckled to imagine what my father would have thought about Josef. Some people marry someone like their dad; I guess I didn't have a chance to find out what he was really like, because I was still a kid when he died. He seemed so upright, indignant about these new-fangled ideas: "Gimmicks, gimmicks, that's all they are!" But Josef; he was a cobbler of gimmicks, and what glee when he devised an outrageous solution. The dashing away of protests: "Whatever works! Don't knock it!"

But he could be so infuriating. He just couldn't imagine what it's like to be a woman. He didn't talk to my mind, he talked to me as his mate.

My friend Michelle said, "It's high time we take ourselves seriously. That old fun and games is <u>out</u>. And who should take us seriously first is our husbands."

Josef just couldn't get his head around this. He said, "Of course I take you seriously. You're my wife! What do you think is more serious than making children? Come on, let's make another one."

Honestly, I could spit with frustration. So I pounded him, just pummelled him. And that made it worse. Because it's awfully hard to resist someone who's holding you down and laughing and kissing you everywhere. So I wasn't very successful in raising our relationship to a new level. He was so sure that the world is a sunny place. You struggle bravely in the storms and celebrate when you survive. Everyone has a part, and when we share our work and make a good time, we're happy. He was delighted with my cooking, he adored his children, he ranted against some of his clients but he used whatever charm or persuasion to complete the job, and then he had this uncanny ability to brush off the dust and laugh, and look all bright-eyed at the next project. It was the same with mountains. And I knew he would kill for me. That's quite an endearing trait.

I've often wondered, though, why I felt the need to keep in touch with Conrad. I think it was because my life with Josef was so predictable. With Conrad I was always puzzling, and alert to his reactions, which in a peculiar way was exhilarating. I knew that under the surface, there were many layers of him. And if I wasn't careful, he'd withdraw. I'd lose him for awhile and I'd have to try hard to please him again. Then he'd give me a little sign: the way he'd smile with his eyebrows going up, or in his letters, when he'd say, "keep having fun." That's what it was. It was the challenge of making him happy, and it was so fleeting, because of the melancholy that lay just beneath the surface.

Whereas Josef <u>was</u> happy, and included me. I was his choice, his icon of woman that he lavished his maleness on. I gave him the unending purpose of providing for his family and sharing his happiness with his friends and an ever-widening community. But in a way, Michelle is right. It wasn't <u>me</u> he took seriously, it was his own idea. But fortunately I had some personal freedom inside me. And the idea of Conrad, even when it was only letters, was complicated and tantalizing. He was always just out of reach. I'm amazed at the power his restraint has over me. Or was it the potential of what he could give me? No, that wasn't it. I wasn't out to get something. It was wanting to relieve that pain of his having to withdraw. What's that need in him that I've wanted to ease? It made me a bit of a clown – dancing around – trying this, trying that. I hate to admit it, but it's almost like a goofy dog trying to please its master. Heavens! Could I be like that? The other quality, that I've admitted before, that he brought out in me, was mothering.

But why go into all of this? Is it strictly necessary? Conrad would find this very undisciplined. Like going on and on about the hotel food. "Marian, what are you fidgeting around for? Just eat what you know is healthy, and then forget food. Concentrate on what we have to do."

No. I've got to watch over myself if I'm going to stay alive. If I don't pay attention to everything, the cancer will slip back and it'll swallow me. The doctors told me, if it recurs, especially somewhere else like my bones or liver, then I'm on the way out. Like Michelle. Her last weeks don't bear thinking about. Though everything was done so thoughtfully. The hospice staff were like family. She showed me what's not going to happen, if I can prevent it. Then, what would happen to my kids? It's all about mothering.

Mothering is not a state of being; it's a response, really. It comes from somewhere deep. Learning the theory and applying the clinical practice of caring loses a lot in the translation. In fact that doesn't even touch what's going on. The crux of it is waking in the night to the cry. The baby's cry, only for mum. There's a compulsion, a panic, to find that cry, grab that baby, give it your breast, relieve its need. What a relief for you both. It's not both, though. It's one. You become part of that baby, the whole world of its survival. Everything you do is generating continued life for your baby. And she or he can't tell you what the agenda is. You have to catch what clues you can pick up. The subtlest changes in sleep breathing, or expression, or stirring in the crib become vital messages. The closest Conrad and I came to that was in the Royal ICU. When you feel an urgency to relieve someone's need, there is no thought for yourself. It's somehow obscene to think of what you want under those circumstances. "Oh, yeah, this precious person may be breathing its last with a raging fever, but I think I'd like a chocolate bar." How ridiculous.

Conrad knew what caring for others means. But there's a difference. When you're a mom, there's no end to it. At least not for me so far. The cry stops, the milk is given. But only for a little while. And you learn to expect it, you want it. You wake up before the cry: where's the baby? why isn't she crying? what's happened? Your breasts long to give their milk – they're weeping their milk, giving, giving. It's supposed to be a joy. And it is. But it's exhausting. Always trying to figure out what to give. As the kids get older, they're leaps and bounds ahead, and contemptuous of yesterday's gifts too. "Oh come on, Mom. We hate Smurfs… or "pop tarts"… or going downtown shopping." I give up. No I don't. I've got to mother myself.

That sounds exhausting too. But I'm being forced to look at things differently. I'm not living at this moment to be of use to other people, certainly not Conrad Falk. And maybe all this trying to care for everything in sight, including myself, is part of the problem. Oh, wouldn't that be wonderful, to walk somewhere with absolutely no obligation. To breathe the perfumed air, to roll in grass like I was three years old again. To forget that I was ever sick. Or left alone by anyone. Being alone could be a chance to dip down into who I've been before. Maybe I could just tack on what I am now. Or absorb it into a fluid shape that's connected to any world I'm in. Maybe there's some new kind of future. Maybe this desert is not outside me; am I hypnotizing myself? Am I losing touch with what's really going on?

Was I really working with Dr. Wei last week? Did we really stand by the windows watching the spring rains as we discussed our patients? Did we really walk through the wards together, greeting the mothers perched on their child's beds? Did he really translate for me so I could enter the world of somewhere so different? Am I doing that now, translating for myself so I can make it back to my own world?

The obligation to please Conrad, to mother him, to love him, is slipping away. I've continued to think of him in the present tense. But really, he's in the past now. I have to trust that he'll be okay. He left me, so he doesn't need me any more. We're free of each other. There's something I have to say, that's almost a vow: if he did return, I would have to not say hello. I would have to say goodbye again. The boat has been cut loose. It is drifting into the distance. But how do I prevent that destructive yearning from consuming me? That grief that goes on and on? The turning back to look behind? How can I learn to trust my own thinking instead of his? This time I will not apologize for all my flaws. Flawed body, flawed mind. No more leaning on a partner. I'll have to dig down inside and keep myself company. And find some way of bidding Conrad farewell.

A little while after Josef died, Conrad phoned me for the first time. It was a shock, hearing his voice again.

May 19th , 1978.

"Hello."
"May I speak with Marian Zabiuk?"
"Yes, speaking."
"Marian, it's Conrad. Are you all right?"
"Conrad… just a minute…okay. I just had to sit down. Where are you calling from?"
"Home, in Halifax. I'm so sorry. About Josef. Are you okay?"
"Oh…thank you. Thank you for the flowers."
"You're welcome. Can I do anything?"
"No. No, we're fine."
"I'm coming out West. I'd like to come to see you. … Marian, are you there?"
"Yes.. I'm here."
"There's a respiratory congress in Portland coming up. I could visit you again afterwards, for a few days. Are there buses up to Whistler?"
"Oh Conrad, I don't know what to say."
"Would you rather that I didn't?"
"Oh, no, it's not that. I can't think. I'm sorry. It's okay at times. I go to work. I look after the kids. But other times… like this."
"I understand. Don't talk if it's too hard."
"It's not that I don't want to see you. It's just that I don't know what it'll be like. For you to visit, I mean. I wanted you to come for so long. I would want things to be nice for you."
"No, no. I'm making this visit for you. Maybe lighten things up a bit. Something else to think about. I'd like to meet Connie!

How about if I call you from Portland, and if you'll have me, I'll come up?"

"Okay. Are you sure?"

"Of course I'm sure."

"When is the congress?"

"July tenth to fourteenth. So shall we say the fifteenth, for a few days?"

"Okay. I'll explain about the bus when you phone."

"Now, if you have second thoughts, just call me here. Have you got a pen?"

"Hmm, where is it?... okay, yes?"

"Area code 902, 276-4590."

"Got it."

"Now Mari, remember. You'll be okay. Call me anytime, won't you ...Mari?"

"Yes. Con, thank you. This means a lot."

"All right now. Don't forget. I love you."

"Oh, Con... same here."

"See you soon. Bye, bye."

"Bye. Con. Thank you."

He was kind. He understood. Everybody seemed to understand. All of a sudden I was in a new club, a secret society that I'd never noticed before: the widow club. Before, I'd been in the physio club, and the mother's club. But all that was bearable. And I'd wanted to learn about them. Learning was built into clubs like that. Curiosity was easy because those worlds were looking forward. But this? No thanks, I didn't want to belong to the new tribe. Why did I want to experience that pain as something new, mine only? All sorts of people came up to me with knowing reassurance, "It'll get better, Marian. Time heals." Go away. I don't want to be weighted down with your grief as well as my own. I don't want to know how you did it. I don't want to be grateful <u>any more.</u>

I waited for Josef. I was like the dog, waiting every day on the driveway for us to come home. Living in hope. My mother said, "Pull yourself together, sweetheart. There's still a lot of living to do." There's still a lot of duty to do, you mean. I didn't hear what else she meant, not then. I remember thinking, I've mostly done what she told me to do... though not good enough. Is she made of tougher stuff? The good old pioneering days of Canada when nobody knuckled under. "Carrying on," not succumbing to the fatigue of it. It's the woman's version of going into battle. Maybe you gradually build up your endurance. Like an athlete. Okay, I can play the game I'm supposed to. I won't bother people by being a spectacle, by tearing my hair and screaming "Josef! Josef!" to the mountains far away. I'll keep that for the night when no one sees me hunched up against his pillow, curled in the smallest knot I can be to squeeze my pain inside me. I am a woodbug, rolled up, rocking, rocking, listening to a strange whimpering somewhere. My mind is supposedly my own, but my body was his. My body and his body: what use now? Gone forever. What on earth am I going to do with my body? Well, it's obvious. Put it to the service of our children. This is all of him that's living now. I can work so hard that his children will flower and be a bouquet on his grave. They will have children and he'll be in them too. I won't be taking anything away from other people to do this, because my work is giving to other people. I try to figure out what they need and use my body to make theirs stronger. It's a perfect solution. People, including my mother (and my father, who lives so much in her thoughts), will approve of this plan: it's a positive and mature approach to this hysterical grief. What would Josef think? He'd kid me. He'd say something outrageous like, "Hey, Doll! Find yourself another guy! (Not Conrad though!) Not too soon, nobody as cute as me. But, go for it!" No, no and no. That door is shut; I'll never open myself up to that again.

Now the sun is high "in the blue, blue sky". I'm getting so thirsty. I must have fallen asleep beside the wheel. Where're the car keys? I'm always losing keys! They're such a nuisance. There must be a store somewhere around, or a cafe. Normally, I'd look for a stream for a quick drink. But I haven't seen a body of water for a very long time. In China water is usually rice plants awash, or metal urns around the hospital for making tea. In the mountains, there were those lovely gushing rapids leading into that pond, where Sun Yat Sen swam, with the light trickling through the lacy trees down to ferns and little purple orchids. Appearing from a bend in the path were the drifting figures of bald monks humming some mysterious chant as they waved in and out of their temple incense. Even in Communist China. But there's none of that here. Only dust and recollection. Nothing of substance to hang onto. And the only purpose is to find a glass of water. At least I haven't run out of gas.

Writing letters wasn't enough any more. I had to hear his voice.

August 3rd, 1978.

"Conrad Falk here."
"Oh, hi, Con. Am I disturbing you?"
"No, no of course not."
"Well, I just wanted to call, to find out if you got back okay."
"Yes, fine, a good flight, once it got airborne."
"I'm sorry about all the hitches."
"No, no, it was a nice visit. A letter's in the mail."

"Well, I thought we'd have had more time to talk. You know, when it's been so long. But that's how it goes, I guess, with kids around."

"Yes, of course. It was great to see them."

"Well, they thought you were fantastic, like a movie star. Hans took your remote control car for show-and-tell. He was so proud of it. Did the photos of you and Connie turn out?"

"They're still in the camera, I'm afraid."

"She wasn't at her best. She's turned all shy with people she doesn't know. Con, thank you for trying to cheer up Emily."

"Oh, it's nothing."

"No, I really appreciate it. I thought it would be better this time. But she's taken the loss of her daddy very badly. I'm quite worried about her. It's so hard to help her."

"Yes, I'm sure it is."

"Are you sure I'm not holding you up?"

"No, no, I have a few minutes."

"Oh, okay. I got the car fixed. It was something in the transmission. You must think we're always hitchhiking up and down the highway."

"We'll get to the alpine another time."

"Yes! I hope you'll come again, maybe in the ski season. Could you bring Andrew over this winter?"

"Possibly. We may be off to Barbados though."

"Oh yes, that's a great break for you. The staff at the clinic were really happy to meet you. It must seem like small potatoes compared to the University. Maria's been trying your new splinting materials."

"Good. Marian, I'm afraid I'll have to fly. I have some classes to prepare."

"Oh, sorry. Well, look. Thanks for coming out to see us. We'll keep in touch, okay?"

"Yes, we'll do that. Bye, Marian."
"Okay, Conrad. Bye."

He kind of slipped away after that. And I can see why. His life was so much more glamorous than mine. It was harder to talk to him, somehow. If the kids had been more open to him, maybe he could have got interested in them. They're Josef's kids, and I guess it showed. My petty little concerns seemed so remote from his life of expert clinical care, teaching – and partnership with another man.

I let things get to me. Leaving the kids every day with the preschool mums was irksome, but it shouldn't have been. They were super kind to do it. Yet I always felt rushed: get everything ready on time, pay them back somehow. For some crazy reason, I began to get jealous of other people being with my children. I started to lose a handle on how to care for them: the ins and outs of what they like to play with their friends, their little disasters in the playground, what they trade with each other. Food became a chore: getting home to all the clatter, and having to scare up something from the fridge. Day after day. We got round the month – barely.

After the move back to Vancouver, I thought it would be easier, having better wages at the rehab clinic. The house sold amazingly fast. The new people wanted to get in for Christmas, to ski over the holidays. It was quite a flurry, to say the least, and terribly hard leaving it all: Josef's carving and beautiful mortice and tenon joints, and the beams that he sweated with all his climbing buddies to hoist up. His union helped me out a lot, but things were getting so much more expensive as the kids got older. I knew the Whistler clinic was going to expand but I couldn't wait around for full-time work there. On the strength of the Bobath courses, and my experience at the Royal, and all that splinting that Conrad steered me into – and having kids too I guess – the rehab clinic took me on.

I thought having Mum to look after the kids would be perfect. But it was worse. I had to protect them from each other. My mother wanted to raise the standards and the kids wanted to have their life the way it used to be. I had to be really careful not to pile too much on her plate. It seemed sensible to add things little by little onto mine. I took pride in how efficient I could be, Daytimer my trusty companion. Sometimes it was a big challenge to get a day to finish. Not that I wanted much time to sit around and think. Or feel. It was all so complicated, and impossible to explain to Conrad. I couldn't expect him to understand. Anyway, it didn't have anything to do with what our relationship had been.

So what we had in common then was physio. That was worth a lot. Do all workers have such an insatiable capacity for shop-talk? I guess each profession has its own language. It's so relaxing to slip into the physio-talk, where we all know just what we're saying. We had a make-over artist come to the rehab clinic soon after I got there in '82. He leapt around the board room facilitating us, mentoring us (or whatever they call it) about our mission and vision and strategic plan. I watched him talking, mouth moving a mile a minute, eyebrows and lips dancing in his face, and I couldn't catch what on earth he was up to. His words didn't hang together for me. It was like a foreign language. We'd leave with our information packages and activity schedules and smile wanly at each other. Could we please just get back to the real work, the real talk? Occasionally at a party, a bunch of us would be stuck in, about some little detail of splinting, whether to make a footplate first or just mould the arches directly on the patient – then we'd realize the husbands were standing around bored out of their minds, like we'd be when they're all discussing the politics of hockey. Women are used to withstanding boredom longer, having had so much more practice.

With Conrad it was very handy, to have physio in common. That tided us over when our friendship was thin on the ground. And the role of clinical advisor was dear to his heart. I could get close to him that way, solving some important clinical problems. Even though I didn't listen, or hear everything he told me because of my newly anxious ways. Maybe it was because of the terrible hole left by Josef, that I seemed to be developing a compulsion to phone him about my troubles.

February 3rd, 1984.

"Hi, Conrad."

"Oh hi, Marian. How're you doing?"

"Con, can I ask you about a patient? I'm going a bit squirrely with this one."

"Sure. What's up?"

"She's a head injury from a car accident. She's 15, on a joy ride with some guys. She's the most beautiful girl. She has hair like you, a mane of curls that glint red, and a beautiful figure. But apart from that, she has a sweet nature; she looks at me with trusting eyes like robin's eggs. I'm teaching her to walk again. The doctors gave her a high priority status, so I see her every day, usually in the parallel bars. We work on weight transference through the hips."

"How's her balance?"

"Not good. She's very frightened of course. One day I took her to the pool, so she'd feel supported in the warm water. She says she feels younger, that she's gone back in her mind to when she was little. One of her friends put a sticker on the back of her wheelchair, "Just visiting this planet."

"She'll likely be better oriented soon."

"Yeah, so anyway, we were walking quite peacefully in the pool, when along comes a crowd of her friends, looking through the window and waving. She gradually froze, and stared at me, like a trapped animal. She was revealed, to herself as well as her friends, in her new body. This lovely girl. What's her future going to be? I can't help but think of Emily, the same age."

"You're pretty intensely involved. You'll have to be careful. Remember how close you were to Rosalba and Mr. Dadson. Keep in mind what your role is. What do you want from me?"

"The trouble is I can't cure her. I can only help her to re-enter a scary world. I have to be cheerful and encouraging, to give her hope. I've started dreaming about her. I won't give up on her, but I feel it's getting out of hand. What would you do?"

"You've got to develop some professional distance. Make a meticulous assessment, clear goals, and stick to it. Are there other team members?"

"Yes, the usual."

"Okay. Get them more involved. Document every detail of progress, and show that to her. Get her family involved too."

"Oh, they're far away, up north. We're the experts, who are going to fix her."

"Hmm. Marian, you know your stuff. You know what to do. Don't try to be everybody's saviour. You have a good heart. But as my mother would say, "God will take care of her." You can't sustain yourself if you get this worked up over every patient."

"It's not everyone."

"No, but things sound awfully serious. Why don't you go out more, have some fun?"

"Yeah, well I do, sometimes."

"Everyone has hard times."

"Yeah that's right. Even you?"

"Of course, even me."

"Conrad, it's good to talk to you. How are you, anyway.?"
"Fine, fine. Take it easy. Call me anytime, okay?"
"Okay, thanks."

I didn't get his message. I didn't listen to anyone else either. I told myself my children were more than enough: I had such a big gap to fill in for them. I could never do enough. It's strange how you can train yourself to work through the heaviness of every day, pull out a way (from somewhere) to do over and over what is required. Treadmill. Martyrdom. Rut. Any definition will do. Years came and went. I hardly have a photo or a memory to recall those years. Was it an uphill path, or a decline? On the outside, I guess we all managed fine. But inside, sickness was sneakily getting rooted in.

I got lost then, and I'm lost now. On the map it looks easy, but it isn't. My vision seems to be altered. Not blurred, because the air is so clear. Not obscured, because there are no trees or cliffs to hide the distant view. It's the way the road disappears into the flatness that's the problem. It twists and is gone.

I left the car on the shoulder of the road, scaled a fence, and walked to a slight rise of land, to see where this road is headed. Instead, beached against a fractured rock, skewed in the sand, I found a skeleton. It wasn't as big or bulky as a cow; maybe it was a deer. The vertebrae were still articulated, and the ribs sprang off like a staff of music, in neat rows. The neural canal had opened into a row of whole notes, and one of the iliac crests lay imbedded in the sand to form a bass clef. The long bones were strewn about. Shreds of flesh still clung to the ribs and vertebrae. There was no skull. The arabesque curve of the skeleton's position suggested a wave, or even a dancer. I kneeled down to examine this echo of life exposed. The living deer materialized before me, its sleek reddish-brown form leaping over a vast plain. I sensed a faint shadow flickering over us, and I looked up to a large bird arcing in the cobalt sky. Except that its head was black, it resembled the eagles that live on our coast. It banked in a wide circle and the arched wings, with tips feathered up, took the form of Conrad's eyebrows when he smiles. Bending my head, I let the tears come. There was no use denying my sorrow.

After some time I raised my eyes to look for the mountains. They were there all right, still far away and blue. Now is the time to develop a different way of seeing.

Maybe I'll have to smell out the way to get there. Or feel my way. That's a phrase we used to use as kids in the dark, when you put your hands out and your fingers waved like anemone tentacles, not knowing what you'd be touching. At Halloween we called it the Torture Chamber. The "hosts" would lead the blindfolded victims through all the horrors we could devise. We told our "guests," usually gullible smaller kids, to put their hands in this tray, of peeled grapes that were really eyeballs, or cold noodles that were really guts, or juice that was blood. We'd tell them to feel their way. Why are the innards of a person so ghastly to touch, or imagine? And a ghoulish thrill for kids? We cackled and shrieked like witches, until the poor little kids were reduced to jelly. Then it was a big success.

Now I'm learning to feel my way solo. My innards are at stake for the second time around. This time it's not my body that's at stake, it's my mind. Or my heart. Maybe my heart's the enemy, leading me astray. My heart doesn't want to be alone. It's always trying to accommodate to whoever's around, even though the push-pull of being with someone is so draining. It used to be that we all had a hope of understanding each other. We moved together as a tribe: eating from the same land, herding the goats across the same river, sleeping in the same tent.

But now, the silences between us are unreadable. So we try to bridge the gap with words, and questions that we hope the other people will answer honestly. But what if the words mean slightly different things, or cloak an altogether different meaning? Then we're thrown back on more primitive methods, and our animal selves take over. I thought I was all organized, set for life. But I must have missed something, about how to survive. The words I'd listened to didn't tell me I could be so sick and not know it. Now I know, that life and death are for animals. And that's what I am. I'll learn what animals do to survive. It has nothing to do with the rules of civilization. It has a lot to do with love.

How I craved love after my surgery. I looked for it everywhere, in flowers on my windowsill, in snatches of music, in sunsets, in hugs from my children. Ordinary simple love. I thought we had a kind of love: Conrad and Marian. Now my heart's tired. It wants to find a resting place. I don't want to wrack my brains to figure out what he wanted, or what anyone else wants. Even at work, before we went to China, I should have thanked my staff for their sympathy about my cancer, sought their companionship, stood on my head like before, to be accepted and part of the group. But instead, I had a hunger for the peace of following my own path. It became imperative not to interrupt my quest toward health for anyone – except my kids, they were worth the risk of neglect.

But Emily said, "Mum, the best thing you can do for us is to get well. Don't worry any more about us. If you learn how to get well, and do it, then that's the best for us. We don't want you to sacrifice yourself and then die. What good is that?" Oh, my beautiful baby. At last, permission to stop the endless effort of searching how to care for other people, especially my kids.

It was a huge shift in orientation. To wake up not thinking: I have to get up, I have to get out there and make food, pack supplies, drive here and there on time and worry about everything. What else should I be doing, what effect am I having on these children, patients, mother, friends? I can never get it all done, can't sit around over lunch. Got to grab a coffee, a chocolate bar, a bag of chips for the car on the way to the next appointment, vary the music tapes in the car according to whether I need keeping awake at the end of the day, or calming down in the traffic jam over the bridge home. This all sounds so self-pitying. But the uncanny thing is, it all seemed normal and regular then, what everyone was living. It certainly didn't seem dangerous. Medical people still wouldn't call it that. But when it stopped, I looked back on it as a crazy trap that I'd got myself into.

If it hadn't been for Michelle I wouldn't have had the luxury of analyzing all this. It would have been too late. As it was for her. It vaguely entered my consciousness, what she was up against, when she came down from Whistler and stayed with us while she was having her chemo and radiation. I was running on my usual track, but one evening we sat on the couch after the kids were in bed and she told me the whole story. Because she was so young, still in her thirties, she thought the pain under her arm was some gland thing. And like me, she was too busy to think of herself. So, by the time she went to the doctor, the cancer was firmly entrenched in her lymph nodes. So much so that they couldn't do surgery right away. Unfortunately she couldn't stop work: there were no benefits from the store. The chemo ground her down though at first she welcomed it, calling it her "pink army", and took the anti-nausea pills to the minute. She tried to eat well but food became an aversion. She described with a certain black humour how her hair fell out, and we had quite a hilarious afternoon in Chinatown finding her a wig. She took the relaxation classes and the healing touch, like I did, but she didn't have enough time. She couldn't sleep in the afternoon; she had to slog on.

One afternoon in the kitchen, while we were making her vegetarian lasagne recipe, she said "Isn't it wild what you can get used to? My first time in radiation, I figured – Michelle, you've landed on a new planet. The machine was definitely a space ship. And these chirpy aliens pushing me into positions I never thought human beings could go. Staring at the little red light. Bang! I'm going to turn into stars. Clothes off; clothes on – you get to be a quick change artist. Strip for the big machine. Now, I waltz in there, pass out the valentine hearts, shoot the breeze with my old buddies, the radiation girls, like it's all a normal day. Marian, keep a watch on my kids, okay? I don't want to put a big trip on you. They think you're really neat, that's all."

Back then, she urged me to have a mammogram but I was always too busy. I'd heard it wasn't the most pleasant test, and it was just one more thing on the list. Finally, I got around to it. Later, when the doctor's office phoned me to come in, I'd forgotten all about it. I thought, oh bother, another pap smear. The only time I darkened that door was to deal with Hans' asthma or Connie's vaccine and broken arm, or Mum's diabetes. I never really liked the doctor but that doesn't matter. He looked his usual stern self, monosyllabic as usual. But he sat down next to me in his examining room, which was unusual. He measured his words.

"Marian, I've received your breast screening report. There was some delay over the holidays. There appears to be a suspicious finding. So we will have to go to the next stage."

"What does that mean?"

"First, I'll examine you to see if I can feel anything; then we'll send you to a more specialized lab. Then we'll take it from there."

"Okay, no problem."

Right, I can handle this. I know about these things. The lab waiting-room was full of morose-looking women, one even snuffling tears. What a bunch of namby-pambies! Where's their backbone? Where's their pride? I'm sure this can all be slotted into place – just take one step at a time. Another mammogram: very nice technician, gentle and obviously used to squeezing every shape and size of breast into her clamping machine. Then the tiny technical room with more machines, X-Ray light box and fancy looking computer. And a gnome-like woman with very thick glasses and a hunched, introspective posture, as she ran the ultra-sound head all over my breast and watched her screen. She spoke so quietly I could hardly hear her.

"I have no doubt that you have a lump in your right breast. Do you see it here, on the screen?"

"Hmm, I guess so."

"A lot can be done, and I'd advise that we start right away. I think I'll call Dr. Hepburn now, Marian. Then we can arrange your treatment together. Is that all right with you?"

"Sure, whatever it takes."

"I'll lay out the various options for you, and I'd like you to see a surgeon in the next few days. We'll take a biopsy so we know what we're dealing with. Here's my card. If you have any questions, feel free to call me."

Big questions or little questions? No question about it. I had to follow very rational and orderly steps along the path of learning to be a cancer patient, victim, survivor or whatever word is designated for that tribe.

The system moved fast. The first step was hearing what the surgeon, Dr. Lorenzini, had to say. "Yes, it's a high grade tumour. I'll decide when I get in whether to do a resection or a mastectomy, but I think I'll take the lymph nodes. I have a spot for you on Friday."

At the door, he put his big hand on my shoulder and spoke straight into my eyes. "We'll look after you, Marian. You've done your part. You got yourself here and that's the important thing. Bravo."

I decided to tell Conrad afterward, and put off telling my mother till the last minute.

"Oh Mum. I'm wondering if you could come and stay with the kids next week?"

"Oh are you going to be away, dear?"

"Well, not away. But in hospital. I have to have a little surgery."

"A little surgery? What do you mean?"

"I don't know how to say this. Don't worry, it'll be okay. It's just a small lump. On my breast."

Silence. "Which one?"

"The right."

"Oh Marian, come here." And she rocked me, just like she used to. It turned out she was a brick. Didn't scold me any more, didn't cry or rush around. Just said, "We'll meet this together, whatever comes. It's part of life."

What a surprise. I had thought I was betraying her, getting sick out of turn. The kids were wonderful too, hugging me all the time. It was a big shock for them so my friends rallied round. It was the same with the people at work, bringing me flowers, sensitive cards, assurance that there was lots of time: the patients and families were all looked after. For once there was nothing I had to do, people cared about me for free, I didn't have to jump through any hoops. The strain disappeared.

I was still naive though, about the implications of my diagnosis: the first news is just the beginning. The other news is that

Josef's presence began to visit me, like an angel. It came out of the blue, a sense that he was perched on my right shoulder, like an owl, whispering in my ear. Honestly! Isn't that just like him?

On surgery day, I joined the little herd of patients at the hospital admitting desk in the lobby. The South Asian man had an entourage with him, even at that ungodly hour: women in brightly-coloured saris, a babe in arms, a little boy holding a young man's hand. Their beauty lit up that austere polished space around the clerk who was stuck in manfully for the onslaught of people like me. Upstairs, the waiting room wasn't so polished: rather, a nether region of doped looking men slouched over Styrofoam cups of coffee. I closed my eyes on that room and heard Josef on my shoulder whispering to me, "Hey doll, don't sweat the small stuff." I drifted into the early days at Herring Cove, lying on the dock with rain beating down on me, washing away the dirt and all the painful thoughts. Time merged everything into the present.

A nurse taps me on the shoulder. "Here's your gown. Could you change here, in the washroom? Your bed isn't ready."

What, with all these men around? Josef whispers, "They're just human beings, my peach. We're all in the same boat."

Then I follow the nurse to the ward, carrying my bag of clothes in my skimpy blue gown, like an exposed tourist. (Oh well, already I'm beginning to shed my pride.) I stuff my clothes in the locker and stand at the windowsill. People are starting off to work. Someone is pulling their kid along to school. A pigeon sits outside, staring in at me.

The time for my surgery comes and goes. The nurse gives me my surgical booties and looks at her watch. "The slate will be piling up. What's keeping them?"

We peek out into the hall. Here comes Dr. Lorenzini, puffing along in his green rumpled surgical scrubs. "All right! Let's go!"

I venture, "I thought you'd be doing your scrubbing."

"Scrubbing? No time for scrubbing. I have to escort my patients to their appointments!" He takes my arm. "She'll be back by noon if I have my way," he tosses to the nurse as we hurry along, me skidding in green booties. "Come along my dear, we've got work to do."

"What happened, Dr. Lorenzini?"

"Well, well, we thought it must be a fire drill. The elevators have shut down. But it seems the union boys are on a work-to-rule, checking all the elevators with meticulous precision. Here we are. Now, shall we wait or take the stairs? No, no, that wouldn't do. We'll wait a minute or two."

A pause. What do you talk with your red-faced surgeon about, before your date with him? "Do you have holidays this summer, Dr. Lorenzini?"

"Holidays! Heavens, no! My son's getting married. Sophia, my wife, is inviting the whole of Italy. I'll be doctoring 'til I'm 90! Here, Marian. Forgive me. You'd better hop on this stretcher. Make it more official. Those ruffians have finally got the thing in working order!"

So he wheels me into the elevator like a proper porter and up we go to the surgical theatre. It's so bizarre. In my horizontal view of the bright lights, tables of equipment, nurses flitting in and out of my visual field, I feel like a sacrificial animal. A kind face puts the anaesthesia mask over me. Now all I've got is Josef's voice in my mind, and then nothing.

When I wake up my right chest is padded up with bandages. I wonder if Dr. Lorenzini has my breast on a tray. Like a big peeled grape. He won't be laughing though. He and I are conspirators in an intimate kind of game. A form of gambling.

When I look under the bandages, I'm repulsed. For all my training and problem-solving skills I'm just an ordinary woman. It's ghastly; it's unreal. The women in the three other beds are trading stories, each one relating valuable survival data. Adalou, the country singer, is definitely going for breast reconstruction, because she has to look good on stage. She knows she's got a big future. Mrs. Boulanger has faith that God will carry her through, even though her cancer is some rare kind that will almost certainly recur in a big way, somewhere else. Tara has two little kids; she's got her husband and friends researching everything in sight so when her surgeon gives her the okay, she'll get right onto it. She's got to get this behind her as fast as possible. It's lights out, like at camp. I put my pillow over my head so the others won't hear that I haven't got as much courage as them. After a while, I have a night visitor.

"Hey, Doll! It's your old husband! So what's with this moaning and sighing? You wanna trade your life for one piece of you? A pretty cool piece, I must admit. But hey. You gave all our babies what they needed. Think of all the poor chicks that never got that chance. And never got me either, to have a whack of fun. Look, Punkin Pie, we had a ball. Who needs it? You're just as gorgeous without it. Keep your life, baby. For me. For the kids. Just you fight, and keep your life. Real safe."

"Josef, I still can't say no to you, and you're damned right."

(His presence hovering beside me, watching over me in my healing, gave me the strength to take charge of what I had to do. After a few months he dissolved, back into my memories.)

At last. Instead of those slick puddles vibrating where the road meets the horizon, that retreat like a dream when you try and try to remember, there's a bump ahead that doesn't disappear. A shed? A barn? A gas station? Yes, and a store. The same colour as fences, fields, and the dusty shoulder of the road: mud brown mixed with sun on silver. A few old signs decorate the facade: Coke, O'Henry, Texaco. Some rusty tilling machinery is scattered along the side. And by the screen door, a cow skull is planted with a few hardy flowers. Over it, a thumb tack pins down a small notice: "Jill Queen's Creek Pottery." A real oasis.

The screen door bangs and I'm inside. It's dark, and there's the heavenly touch of a cool breeze coming from somewhere. Heading toward it, I realize it's the cooler for drinks. Oh joy. I open the door, and put my hand around a can of 5-Alive. The cold is almost burning. I give each hand a turn, on half a dozen cans. Then I spy one of iced tea. I grab it. I hold it to my forehead, then each cheek, over each ear, and finally, the back of my neck. I snap the metal tab and tip my head back. The sweet cold wetness fills my mouth, especially my tongue, with an undercurrent of lemon and bitter tea. It's almost too much. In the gloom at the back, behind the cooler, a pair of eyes is watching me, surrounded by glinting jars or pots. I let the cooler door slam to, and carry my can over to the counter. The owner of the eyes gets up and comes round to me. She pings in the sale and we look at each other. She's a lot taller than me, stringy, with trailing greyish-brown hair pulled back, a thin face, long sinewy neck, big hands with veins and tendons criss-crossing under her skin. She turns back to her dim alcove, and I follow. There're some boards laid out with bricks between, and balanced along in arrangements of tall, squat, round, and square are the pots, made of clay or ceramic. She takes a round jar with a wavy lid over to the small window, and suddenly the colours gleam at me. Is it celadon blue? Or cobalt? Or aquamarine? All of those, and purple too. I expect Aladdin's genie to leap out. But the jar sits quietly in her hands.

"Did you make these?"

"Yeah."

"They're beautiful."

"Yeah."

I hold up a flat dish with a blue iris etched into the pearly grey. "How did you make this?"

And she explains: it's been a long time, years and years, (more than twenty) since she sat with her master in a Japanese village, and though not understanding his language, watched his hands and laboured through all the stages to assist him in making pots: collecting water in wooden buckets from the icy stream, gathering wood for the kiln, grinding the mineral for the blue glazes that came from a remote region in China, and tenderly handling all the earthen materials, until she too became a master. I am in the presence of another wise woman teacher. I am sunk in admiration for her, and a flood of grief fills me. I take the lidded jar in my own hands. It is cool and perfectly smooth. It is exactly the shape for my hands to hold. It is the vessel to hold all my losses: the loss of my father, of Josef, of Michelle, of my breast, of Conrad. And the loss of my naive self. Now there is no more time for that self. It's time for my life's work, which is here in every moment, to understand what is. It's time to gather my strength.

I'm not lost anymore. My eyes are streaming tears, that fall over the curve of the jar like the silver paths of fishes. Jill Queen is observing me. I cannot give up this jar. I root in my bag and write a cheque to pay for it. She doesn't bother with ID. She looks at me as if she already knows me, and says, "There's a powwow later today. Anyone can go. Follow the signs for the reservation outta here, before you hit the highway. You can camp there if you want."

"Okay. Thanks. And thanks for this."

"Yeah. Take it easy. See ya."

Why not? Why not do what she says? There is nowhere I can't go now. I can do whatever I want.

Outside, it takes a moment for my vision to adjust to the fierce sunshine. In the shadow beside the car, a tiny brown sparrow hops and scratches in the dust, looking for something. He glances at me sideways, his head tilted in a question. I place my jar carefully on the back seat.

The Creek Pottery woman was right: it wasn't hard to find the reservation, with orange signs along the gravel road, pointing: "Pow Wow Saturday." Bells rang out, and around a bend in the dry fields rose a white church with arabesques like giant double commas. There were crowds of people walking from a roped-off parking area toward the church gate. So I followed them, looking for the Pow Wow Ground. The carved doors were open, candles flickered in clusters, and beyond all the heads, the organist played something slow and beckoning. Then the priest began a prayer: some in English, some in Latin I guess, and some in another language. This was a new kind of service for me. Stuffed in the standing crowd at the back, I felt the warmth of all those people; some looked Spanish, or like the Salish from home; others were polished like tourists from good hotels; others with backpacks and scruffy hair. A young girl and an older woman read from the Bible. A small choir of kids with black hair and blue tunics sang a hymn that everyone seemed to know. A mixed bag of voices filled my head with benediction. Then the priest began talking to us about sin and penitence so I slipped away to look for the powwow. It wasn't far. The bleachers were *edged around with a string of plastic flags, jelly bean colours. A girl with hair like a horse's long mane flying in the wind took my ticket money. There was a spot left on one of the lower bleachers. All sorts of people wore all sorts of costumes: tribal outfits, western gear, shorts and T-shirts. An elder was talking slowly on the loudspeaker about brotherhood and sisterhood, about all the tribes coming together for this competition, how certain young people had come back to them from terrible addictions and the suffering of violence and were now earning awards and trips around the country by their championship dancing. He told us we should all seek peace and healing in our lives; all of us should gain strength from each other, Native and Non-Native. Then he spoke in his native Indian language and translators paraphrased his words in other tongues. Drummers at one end of the circle began banging on flat drums with curved sticks, and a spine-tingling cry rose up from the women sitting near them. The procession of dancers was led by a huge man with a white stripe painted across his eyes. His long fingers shook. The eagle feathers in a huge circle on his back swayed as he stamped this way and that. Behind him came women in jingle dresses of intense colours, mainly red and turquoise and black. Some wore shawls embroidered with suns, or flowers, or zig zag lightning. The thousands of silvery jingles jumped on their dresses. Best of all were the tiny children dancing beside their mothers; they didn't have to sit on the sidelines. They reminded me of little speckled fawns prancing, always beside their protecting doe. A cluster of young men leaping with feathers shaking began fanning out and the chief invited everyone to dance. Soon the parade circle filled with young and old, shorts and jeans, buckskin dresses and baseball caps. The guy with the white stripe on his face loomed up and before you know it, he grabs my hand.*

"Come on lady, you're up."

"What?"

"Didn't you hear the elder? Just pretend you've got some jingles on."

What the heck. I start hopping from one foot to the other, round and round in the dust. The drums, with their mythic painted birds, pound as we go by, the women are laying into their chanting like a howling wind, the legs of the jingle dancers are snapping silver, until I'm pulsing in every part of me. It stops. I sit down. I'm in a blur of colour. I'm in colour down to the cellular level. That can't be bad.

It's time to move on, time to get to the mountains. On the way past the ribbon of flags, an old woman is sitting on the ground, with a blanket spread in front of her. I take a closer look. There are rows and rows of necklaces, and bracelets and earrings. Turquoises are set in carved silver, making a pattern of triangles across the blanket. Feathers arranged like a collar look so soft and regal. The earrings are all the colours of the jingle dancers. I reach out for a pair. The woman passes them to me from a hand in the extremity of age. The brown skin is stretched loosely across the large knuckles, the lines and lines of working in the sun are carved there; her nails are ridged but symmetrically square. Her arms, her whole body, are covered with charcoal grey cloth, despite the heat. I've never seen such an old woman in all my life. Her face looks at me from ages past, her hair in smoky wisps around her features of driftwood. The eyes, these long eyes. What have they seen? I think to myself: the mouse woman, the spider woman.

I say "How much are they?"

She points to the ticket. Is she Hopi, Blackfoot, Apache, someone rarely seen or always here? Maybe she doesn't speak English. I thank her and start walking away, but I feel a prick of sorrow, leaving her there on the earth. I turn back and see her *gazing with her long eyes, still black, at the mountains, not so far away now.*

When I wrote to Conrad explaining about the cancer: the aftermath of surgery and getting involved with the cancer clinic and what the specialists told me about my statistical chances: 30% this, 70% that), he sent me a rather odd reply:

…I was very sorry to receive your letter with news of your cancer. It was quite a shock for you, I'm sure. I wish you had let me know earlier; it must be quite a while that you have been dealing with this. I'm enclosing some recent literature that the Head of Oncology here recommended. The more informed you are, the more you can take action. It is most important for you to seek the greatest expertise possible; hopefully, out West there is the highest quality treatment.

I must admit I was not surprised to hear of your illness – a few warning signs have been evident in recent years. I'm so glad that your department has given you leave of absence; take full advantage of it. Andrew joins me in sending best wishes for your recovery. I'm very concerned about your progress – let me know the details.

Love,
Conrad

He seemed kind of formal about it, almost scolding, but I suspected that he was worried about me but didn't want to go overboard with the emotional stuff. There didn't seem much point in reporting back to him about my treatment. I felt kind of private about it, especially the healing touch, the new clothes I had to buy, and remedies such as mushrooms and herbs that I tried. He seemed very far away. The flowers he sent every month or so were wonderful, so flamboyant and glamorous compared to his letters, which showed me how many rungs up the ladder he was ascending, and how I could take advantage of the latest breast cancer research. It was quite awe-inspiring, his publishing record with the University. And he seemed to like the management side. I guess that gave him the opportunity to change the hierarchy to some extent. The Physio Association certainly recognized all his contributions. I wouldn't have wanted to stand in his shoes, though. I certainly relished the leisure to dip into all the alternative treatments around, especially food. For the first time in their lives, the kids had super healthy food: home made juices, tofu and broccoli stir-fries, salmon. I thought, why not blow some of the profits from the house? What's more important than our health? It was getting easier to smooth away the fear of dying.

Barb, my friend in Edmonton, urged me to try yoga, and that put me into a good space. There happened to be an old Herring Cove reunion about that time. We had a ball. There's nothing like jiving with guys who know the same songs as you. I started circulating around more. Old cancer troupers kept coming out of the woodwork. Most of them were great to talk to, no secrets there. The new ones, who wanted advice, put me back into that panicky feeling. I gave them what I felt like doing, but it was a bit close and I learned to say "no" when I'd had enough. You can pass some things on – it's not necessary to shoulder everything. When some colleagues gave me some patients who needed home visits, I found it actually fun, practising my knowledge. I was part of their life as a patient. I had a better understanding of what it's like to receive care. I started watching them carefully – comparing notes. How did they cope with whatever came along? I felt closer to them than before, but more relaxed. After all, we have to find our own path. I actually respected them more, didn't feel I had to save them – they were travelling their own unique trail, just like me, and it was very heartwarming to cross paths.

But I could wave and say goodbye, trust that they'd meet another person to pick it up and give them something else.

It must have been the following March, when Conrad phoned me about the project in Guangzhou:

"Would you be interested, Marian?"

"This has really blown me away! I've never even thought of going to China, let alone work there. How did this all come about?"

"University Hospital has been in touch with one of their alumni, a doctor connected to the UN, for a few years now. He developed a medical relief system for the massive flooding in central China some while back. Now he's determined to jack up the standards of Western-style medicine, and that includes Guangzhou."

"Is it a rehab centre?"

"No, a general hospital. They told me there're no rehab facilities at all. Apparently some enterprising woman has started a one-year course for "middle doctors" somewhere north of Shanghai. Before the Tienanmin massacre the Americans had started something at Sun Yat Sen University, but they pulled out."

"So, Conrad you're a pioneer!"

"In a sense, yes. Just think back to Royal Memorial. An old culture, with a new profession. The Physio Association has asked me to send an abstract for the North American Congress next June. They want us to report on what we accomplish there. We can do it, Marian. Why not come? It's only for four months. You're on leave of absence anyway."

"I don't know if I have the stamina. You know, recovering and all."

"Here's another 'bon mot' from my mother, 'A change is as good as a rest.' It'd be good for you, to get back in the traces.

You have a lot to offer. You've got the experience with kids that would complement what I do. Come on, Mari!"

"I don't know if I could leave my own kids for that long. It's a lot to put on their grandma."

"Marian, you always say how strong she is. Anyway, they're not little any more. Emily could probably look after the whole lot. But perhaps you have misgivings for another reason."

"Well yes... there is that. I was married a long time. I've grown up a lot since then...When do you have to let them know?"

"By Tuesday. Don't think too hard. I'll call you again Sunday night. This is a great opportunity for both of us. We have a lot of backing: the UN, the University, the Association and the Chinese are inviting us. We're not pushing ourselves on them. I know you'll be so glad you did it."

"You're awfully persuasive. Talk to you Sunday then. Thanks for thinking of me, Conrad."

I wondered, Why am I the one? Is this a rehab programme for me, to take cancer off my mind? Strengthen me up? Or does he need me for some reason? Am I some kind of protection, a buffer against something difficult in China? Or does he see some potential in me that I haven't noticed in myself? It was so intriguing, I just couldn't say no. I started thinking about the kids in China, what toys and equipment to take, what books as a basis for teaching. I found a terrific paperback called, "Disabled Village Children", the nitty-gritty of Third World rehab. People started donating stuff. My kids got behind it. The ball was rolling.

PART THREE

REUNION

The drumming is fading away. The purple sky in my rear view mirror is reflected on the mountain slopes ahead, creased by indigo shadows. Night is falling and my destination is near. Like the Creek woman said, I can camp anywhere in this vacant land. My mother's coat and Yuen's shawl should be enough blanket.

This will be a test, because I've never camped alone. Thank goodness I have strong companions in my mind, like Josef and Dr. Wei.

I'm getting awfully hungry. Rolling around the back seat are two hotel oranges; that'll have to do until tomorrow. Here's a tree for shelter…maybe the gnarled remainder of some rancher's hope.

Lying with the stars darting out, one by one, it's not so bad. Heat still rises from the hard ground. A chill wind from the east finds every gap in my wrapping, my second skin. I can't seem to stop shivering. Even my mind is beginning to go numb.

Dark, dark now. Coyotes stagger their howling in rows of icicle notes. My left hipbone begs for relief. I shift over, holding on to my inadequate covers. The tree is not a shelter but a black spectral shape looming over me. A bear.

Oh, Bear, with stinking breath of death. You will get me in the end, that's sure. Is now the time? Not yet. But you're so big and black and hairy. You have sharp, sharp teeth. Go away, Bear! What shall I throw to you, to make you go away? My breast, of course, but that's already gone. My heart? No. You can't have that. Not my heart. I'm just a tiny, insignificant creature. If I roll up into a little ball, maybe you won't find me. I'll hide inside myself, curled round, and you won't be able to tear out my innards. I'll go down, into the deeper darkness, down where the black crawling creatures are sticking out their parched tongues for the tears that are falling from me. Tears that drip into a cave of sorrow from a source up in the air where the wind blows and waterfalls flow from the distant snows fed from the clouds moist and grey. Where the brightness used to be. I miss Conrad. I don't want to lose him. I don't want to be alone. The cavelings scuttle and wait for the shivering tears that seep like exudate from the punctured crust; the pliant encasement of polish, that makes things look good on the outside, for all the world to see. Until the unpredicted moment when it is stabbed by an experience that feels like a death. And the dangerous hurt makes me easy prey.

Barricaded no longer, I see the bear. Can I escape? Am I trapped in this cave by a clamp? Despite my chewing and pulling, am I bound in pain by the teeth of longing for what is gone forever, the trap that I make for myself, over and over? Temporarily quenched, the thirstlings huddle in the darkest cracks. Conrad, it's not your fault. You need to survive too. You escaped from me; that's what you needed to do.

Can I teach the tears to soak into the earth and make a quiet place, where soft green leaves offer a bed to settle into with a sigh? Where I can be anytime I want?

A faint glow in the eastern sky, behind the jagged line of mountains, hints at warmth again. Such a good feeling, to awaken again, warm! To be within reach of what I set out to do!

Before we flew to China on our "joint venture," Conrad and I arranged to meet at the airport. I saw him, waiting for his baggage. He was still so handsome, calm and in control. Easy to admire. Black clothes, from head to toe. Some costly, thick woven fabric for his shirt. Pleats in his smooth pants that followed the strong muscles of his legs. More weight now, prosperity and success, written in the gold accents to this black: a large belt buckle, a wide watch, a signet ring. His hair, now brushed away from his brow, tamed and greying, but still curling old gold. His tanned hands and face alert, quick. I delayed the moment when I had to reveal myself. How often does a person get that chance, to see without being seen?

As I approached him, I felt small and ordinary compared to him, toting my old suitcase from years ago. Maybe he would look down on me. Instead his face lit up. He dropped his bags and reached out for me. Such abandonment! I flew into his embrace. His eyebrows, winging upward, arched over the golden eyes that welcomed me back. He kissed me on both cheeks, continental style. "Mari! How good to see you again!" Yes. How very good. We stood there, drinking each other in. My sensible self re-asserted itself, and I led him to the departure gate, where they charge the 'airport improvement fee.'

Sitting beside him on the plane turned out to be quite cosy. At first we talked about our supplies for work and what the funding groups expected of us. But then we watched the movie, *Top Gun*, and that brought us to trading impressions of other movies. Coincidentally, we were both Jack Nicholson fans. And then we dozed. I even woke up with my head on his shoulder. Oh dear, was that a problem? No, it was all part of being on the road again. He was kind, indulgent of little Marian (not so little any more, and quite a bit lopsided, but definitely on his side, in his camp). He asked me a few well-placed questions, and before I knew it, I was telling him all about my life, mainly my kids, and then because we had so many hours, about my illness. His life, he kept more to himself, just the Caribbean holidays, the interesting work, the cultural scene in Halifax. He loved the symphony, and that part I found hard to follow, what various composers were doing in their music. I asked about Andrew, but that seemed to be private territory. There were the permitted topics, and the forbidden topics. After all, we'd been apart for so long, middle-aged adults now. Not confidantes still wet behind the ears, like before. Yet, we felt so close—his curving smile so close, our hands resting beside each other on the reclining chairs. When our tinfoil-wrapped meal arrived, he gave me his pimento olives that he knew I loved, from the days in Spain. I poured his wine for him, gently, as if I'd been doing it for years.

By the time we got to Hong Kong we were ready to experience things together again. We recaptured the old days of wandering around Europe. We tasted all kinds of amazing Chinese food at the night market, hiked up the watershed to the Peak, joined the working crowds on the Star Ferry. Working friends again. My family back home receded into the distance. This is going to be fun!

Landing in Guangzhou was like returning to the 1950's. After the military-looking customs officers waved us on, and the hospital delegation had gathered us up, we squeezed into the hospital van, and drove through the dark streets. Sparse lighting and no paint on the wooden or concrete buildings and almost no advertising signs made the occasional person standing by a porch or walking on the sidewalk seem like a ghost. Almost no cars, just a few taxis and trucks. Even the air felt brown and moist. There was the sense that the city had been waiting, since 1949, for something to happen. At the sign on the wall of the hospital, translated for us: "Guangzhou People's General Hospital," the driver honked and a tiny woman emerged from her kiosk and opened the wrought-iron gate. Inside, a square formed by the old brick walls opened up between the buildings: our precinct, home in this huge strange city. It reminded me a bit of Royal Memorial, built by the British before the last Dynasty collapsed. The delegation, vice-directors and nurses, shouldered our bags and dragged them up the grey stairs of our residence, past the big wicker baskets full of IV bottles, past the closed grates where family noises and Chinese Opera and smells of cooking told us this was home for many, and finally to our door. First the rattling of keys, excited translations back and forth, and then we were waving good-bye. Dashing to the window, I saw the delegation pushing their heavy black bikes past the gates again, for the night-time ride home.

We chose rooms and met the Japanese technician who was staying for a week to teach the staff how to maintain the cardiac monitors that had been donated and that were now sick themselves. I lay in my new bed, the springs a bit uneven, and gathered the pink flowered quilt around me. There was a smell new to me in this room – what was it?

Ching, ching! woke me up, and what sounded like Chinese Viennese waltzes, and birds chirping in a tree outside my window, then some shrill clanking of metal on metal, interrupted by a shaking rumble of a big truck going fast, a chorus of car horns, and many, many voices and footsteps, all Chinese. I lay listening to these messages, and guessing what the world looked like. At last curiosity tugged me to the window, where I could look down on our part of Guangzhou going to work. Hundreds of bicycles wheeled by, pedalled by hundreds of people with black hair and plastic rain jackets. A woman, the neighbour across the narrow road, up high like me, was watering her potted kumquat tree and what looked like a banana plant, waving in its roof garden next to the electric wires. Some faded red lanterns dangled along an arch over some closed wooden shutters. The sky was a rectangle of grey.

In the common room, someone had left a thermos of tea and some bread and a toaster. Conrad sat at a scuffed little table by the window, reading his notes.

"Good morning, Marian. Did you sleep well?"

While we ate our sweet toasted bread, we began planning – no time to lose.

"The way I see it, Marian, the most important part of our work will be education. These people have been isolated from the world for so long, they have a lot of catching up to do. We'll have a chance to really get in on the ground level and show them what physiotherapy can do."

I thought back to outreach home visiting. That was the model I was used to. Asking a household of people, "What do you want from me? Let's work out what your sick person needs." This sounded more ambitious. Maybe this would be too much for me. I tested the waters a bit.

"Do you think they need support for what they're already doing?"

"Oh, of course, that goes without saying. The staff and families want higher quality care, obviously. There's a window here, that the officials have conceded. Who knows what political strings have been pulled to make this happen. Dr. Yang, the instigator of the whole project, told me in Halifax that it's very important to establish prestige for ourselves. Then the hospital system hierarchy will kick in, and we'll get permission to work with whoever we want."

"That doesn't sound all that Communist."

"In what sense? Remember, it's an authoritarian system."

"But isn't the idea to give power to the people?"

"Marian! Are you still the naive person I know and love? If we want to work with the people, we have to work with the system. I hope you're not going to go all purist on me."

"No, no. It's lucky you found out so much before we got here."

"Planning, Mari. And we'll feel our way. Now, let's make a list of our goals."

The door buzzer announced our first visitor, Nurse Lai, our translator.

We were gung ho. We had our presentation ready. Conrad sent a message requesting an opportunity to introduce our plan for rehabilitation to all the heads of departments. There was a hospital extension phone system and we were told by the administrative assistant that we would be contacted soon to arrange a meeting. We waited the rest of the week, hearing nothing. Nurse Lai took us on little tours of the hospital, but we felt sure we needed official permission before entering the wards.

We ate in the small guest dining room, chatting in basic English with the Japanese technician and the occasional visiting doctor. Conrad was champing at the bit, I could tell, and entering a strong silence. He didn't explain, but I think he felt insulted, to be ignored, not to be lauded as the amazing foreign expert. I thought, there must be a key to open the door, but what is it?

One day, Nurse Lai took us to the outpatient department, on the other side of the open tiled entrance, where two trees grew, with branches and leaves poking up above the partial roof of corrugated tin. They looked like they'd been left over from the forest and forgotten, except for some leaves scattered across the tile. A flood of people filled the corridors and waiting areas: fathers and mothers carrying children, young people leading old people carefully as they shuffled along, some in obvious pain. Some people with IV's in their arm, or in the case of babies, in their scalp, sat on benches, leaning against their caregivers, who held the pole for the IV bag up high. Some leaned on crutches, others on each other. Some babies were bundled in thick quilts, their beautiful faces peeping out. There wasn't one fat person in all those hundreds. Many men were sinewy, slight, and brown, no doubt from hard, hard work. Many older women carried big packages and bags, or babies in a sling. All were speaking in various Chinese dialects. We were surrounded by languages of no relation to our own, not one word.

I felt a flashback to when I was a small child. What was it? … It was sitting on the boardwalk on the edge of the cove. Looking out toward Duck Rock. It was the sea lions gathered in spring for the herring. Voices insistent, persistent, layered over and over.

Ar-unh, Ar-unh, Arunh. Important, but unknowable to me. Life that I was part of, but outside my comprehension. It's soothing having your thoughts drifting within another circle of everyday life. It's almost like being a baby again, before language. A baby expert from the West.

At a raised counter at the end of the hallway sat three nurses in starched caps who waved to Nurse Lai. She introduced us, and there was a lot of joking and laughing. As we walked away, Nurse Lai remarked, "They are very curious about you. They think Dr. Conrad very handsome, like movie star. They wonder if you are married couple. When I say no, they are very interested. They think you are more than colleagues, we say tongsi. Maybe lovers like in banned movies from Hong Kong."

I laughed. "Oh, I can definitely assure you, we are only tong-si." (If you only knew, Nurse Lai.) "Nurse Lai, why are there so many people here? Do they all have appointments?"

"Some only. Many take long journeys in from villages, for special care. It is their choice now. They do not respect village medical service so much. Before, they are not allowed to travel, but now they can. That makes big strain on the doctors here. They see 70 to 100 patients per day, or more. Wait, please. I check in on Orthopaedics. I know nurse there."

We were squeezed into a tiny room, and watched the taping of dozens of children with club feet. The poker-faced orthopaedic surgeon listened to the plight of family after family. The next group in line filled the doorway with curiosity, until periodically the nurse would shoo them away like chickens and bang the door shut. Even then, it would edge slowly open, and faces would peer in again. The doctor's thick, paw-like hand would shove X-rays onto the light box, point with his pen, and occasionally dart a diagnosis our way, in English. Fractures, rickets, arthritis, polio. Nurse Lai struggled bravely with all the terminology, flipping through her dictionary as fast as she could.

"Dr. Zhu says many of his patients he cannot treat properly. He knows what they need, but in poorer villages work unit cannot pay. Or they cannot get to us for changes of splint. Or he cannot get supplies. He wants to know how do you treat these patients." Ah, Conrad, he leapt to attention! He demonstrated exercises to teach a family to carry on at home. But only for a minute, because Dr. Zhu gave a nod to the nurse, and in came another group, clustered around their ailing child, mother, or grandpa.

As we neared the entrance again, Nurse Lai told us, "Always we have two hours for lunch; many staff ride their bicycles long distances to work every morning. We enjoy rest with our lunch."

"Where do you live, Nurse Lai?"

"Oh, I am in female residence for hospital staff."

"Do you have rooms with your husband?"

Her young face tries to look cheerful. "Oh no, there are many nurses in one room. And one bathroom to share. We have not yet been assigned to apartment."

"Will that be soon?"

"Maybe not soon. Maybe a year or more." She puts on her cheerful smile. "But waiting is not so bad. 'No problem!' as you say."

"We must be keeping you from your rest. Where do you go?"

"Oh, in office, or in room behind ward." Her bright open face leaned toward us with a puckish smile. "I like play badminton with my friends, that you met. Always Dr. Zhu plays chess, with Vice-Director Wei."

Conrad smiled at her earnest youthful manner. She needed a rest. "Thank you, Nurse Lai. M'Goi Sai. Marian and I will do a little exploring on Renmin Road, for our lunch break."

That first day on Renmin Road was like Piccadilly Circus. We dashed across through the throngs of bicycles, honking taxis and trolley buses. On the other side was a street restaurant that made hot pots while you wait, so we got one that looked like lasagne, that had eggplant and mushrooms and meat. It became Conrad's favourite dish. In buckets were live fish and shrimp. Say the word and you had a shrimp hot pot. And always Chinese tea.

We turned a corner, and then another, and there was a street market. Metal clothes racks held bunches of dresses, shirts, pants, and jackets. Mao suits seemed to be a thing of the past, except for the older people, perhaps more staunch Communists. Boxes of shoes, and plastic red and blue sandals, were laid out in rows. In plastic basins were little wriggling things. Tiny frogs, trying to hop over each other and over the side, were scooped up in handfuls, or picked over carefully by the discriminating cook. Were they refugees from the rice fields? In a square wire cage sat a furry animal like a beaver, with bent whiskers and dull, exhausted eyes. Passing by the clothes racks we came to a stained wall, where an old man sat in a straight-backed chair with his mouth wide open, and another bent to his task of extracting a tooth. Around them a cluster of onlookers watched intently.

From the corner of my eye I caught a quick movement. A fish taking a mighty leap from its barrel and slithering away! A catfish or dogfish, with long whiskers and a snaky body. Its gills were heaving as it belly-danced down the barren riverbed of street, avoided by bicyclists and chased by the vendor. I wanted to cheer for its escape.

Near the intersection, we passed a clutch of men standing around a small carpet on the ground. I glimpsed part of a tiger paw, but my camera was a threat, and the nearest man pushed me on. (It seems that every species of animal is represented in this city.) Next were the vegetable vendors, standing with their bicycle baskets piled with greens, lotus roots, and mushrooms. Each block had unexpected combinations for sale: machinery parts next to CD's and tapes, underwear next to herbal medicine. Ahead a sign in English and an arrow pointed us to "Chen Family House Museum."

"This building comes from an era long before Communism. Look at the carved stone columns along the veranda."

"Yes, and the tiles along the roof! Ceramic animals and birds: all the creatures from the market. Oh! And dragons and guardian dogs. What are those fierce birds –twisted around each other? Their feathers look like flames."

"Something mythic – phoenixes maybe."

"Like on the totem poles up our Coast. Maybe it's the family clan symbol."

"Who knows?"

"Conrad...do you see those scenes of people, set into the wall? In robes flowing like drapes."

"No doubt composing poetry under their weeping willows."

Inside the façade, dark shadowed rooms surrounded a courtyard decorated with red lanterns and potted flowers. Doors and windows carved like lace let the breeze flow through. Josef would be impressed. Lovely objects inside invited us to look closely: ivory ships and blue curving vases, embroidered coats on poles embellished with dragons, ancient musical instruments with long slender necks. An intimate, faraway world.

"Why don't we sit down for a moment?" Conrad led me to a stone bench in the sun.

"Isn't this fantastic? A collection of old China."

"Yes, it's quite important, collecting."

"How do you mean, Conrad? Are you a collector?"

"After a fashion. I pick up relics from Cape Breton: tools, stuff like that."

"Really! You never told me about that. What've you got?"

"Oh, flotsam and jetsam: bits of ships off the wrecks. Nutmeg graters, old bottles, sail-making tools, lanterns. My pièce de résistance is a saw tooth straightener."

"Like in the market today! You should donate it to the dentist!"

"I hate to think what he uses. Yes, they're like symbols of the old days, a simpler time." Conrad looked down at his hands, spread like fans on his knees. "The wicked 'Four Olds,' or 'Five

Bads,' or whatever it is. Evidence of former decadence, no doubt."

"I wonder who the Chen Family was."

"We'll never know, Mari. Wiped out, probably. In the name of Party Progress."

"Yes…perhaps. What must it have been like, living here with so many generations having gone before, in the same house?"

"Difficult, no doubt. As every family is."

"Was your family difficult, Conrad?"

"Aren't they all?"

"Do you mean, your father not being able to find work that suited him?"

"That, and my mother never letting me forget it. She put her hopes in me, the precious younger one. Pushed me to make up for all that unfulfilled life of my father. An impossible task, I've since realized."

"But you're so accomplished and admired by everyone."

"Nothing's ever quite enough for my mother. Once she spoke about how easy my brother and his wife were with my niece, Stephany. She said, 'That girl has just not been trained.' That's when it dawned on me, I'd been trained, right good. And so had my father. Control was where it was at."

"But both your parents loved you. They've been so proud of you."

"I assume so. My father never had much to say. Like a jar of my mother's crabapple jelly, I'd been thoroughly boiled. Anyway, the lunch break must be over. Let's see what the Guangzhou People's General Hospital has to offer this afternoon."

I almost took his hand. (Strive no more, Conrad. Your mum adored you. She wanted to protect you by teaching you to be so competent that the world can't destroy you. You're good enough.) I had to run to keep up with his long legs striding down Renmin Road back to work.

That evening was our official welcoming banquet. That's the first time we met Dr. Wei Jin Zhan, Vice-Director of Acute Care and Research. Nurse Lai told me not to dress up; banquets are casual, though the food is quite special. So I wore my usual green pants and jacket. Many, many courses arrived on small plates: unidentifiable delicacies. I breathed a quick prayer that the fish escaping down the street wasn't among them. They put me next to Dr. Wei, probably because he spoke English so well, and Conrad at another round table with the Hospital Director and Communist Party group.

It was impossible to decide his age. Dr. Wei would have been a tall man, except for his rounded spine. His extreme thinness gave me the urge to prop him up somehow, like a tree blown over by a storm. But his face was youthful, with no wrinkles or grey hair. He must be about my age. He looked as if he needed this banquet, but instead picked at tiny bits and sat hugging his rumpled lab coat. I realized that though I looked at his face and eyes as we spoke, he averted his glance. Perhaps this was decorum, not to be direct in attention to each other. So I averted mine.

Then, for the first time, he spoke to me in a more confidential way.

"Pardon me please, Miss Merry Ann, for not conversing more. I am preoccupied about one of my patients; he is hanging in the balance, as you say. Would you please introduce me to Dr. Conrad?"

"Of course, Dr. Wei." (I could never be bold enough to call him 'Jin Zhan,' but I had the feeling that he might be camouflaging himself by using those inverted names our staff thought were appropriate. Or…was he even mocking us? No…his expression was so kind.)

It was obvious when they began chatting together that both of them had met his match. Dr. Wei even knew some of Conrad's old friends, from his Toronto days. He graciously invited him to ICU the next day: here's progress! Then the toasts began: Gambai! Gradually the group became jovial, and a Karaoke TV was brought in. Party Director Yao, in her severe grey suit, stood up and marched over to the microphone. On flashed the picture, with words in Chinese. And this Communist Official sang like a nightingale, in a sweet soprano!

Dr. Wei leaned closer to me and spoke in a quiet voice, "She was formerly in the Opera. Would you like to hear this story?" He murmured the tale of how a cloud goddess loved an earthly man, how they endured many trials, and in the end soared into the sky, spirits forever together.

"Thank you, Dr. Wei. I never expected to be enchanted in China."

"Oh, there is much about China that you will not have expected."

The next morning I awoke to the sound of the phone ringing. Oh my gosh, how do I answer it? What do I say? What if it's important and I can't understand a word? Where is the thing anyway?

"Hello?"

"Good morning, Miss Merry Ann. This is Dr. Wei."

"Oh. Good morning, Dr. Wei."

"Am I disturbing you?"

"Ah, no. No, not at all."

"Have you eaten yet? I hope you slept well?"

"Well, yes. Thank you."

"Miss Merry Ann, I have good news."

"Good."

"The presentation for the directors? That Dr. Conrad requested? It is arranged."

"Well, that is good news."

"Yes, it is scheduled for next Wednesday at 2 o'clock."

"Wonderful. This is very important for Conrad. It's gratifying that all the obstacles have been removed so quickly."

"Yes. Quite fortunate."

"Thank you, Dr. Wei. Please pass our sincere appreciation to the people who made this possible."

"Oh, it's nothing."

"I'll tell Conrad about this. Thank you again."

"You're welcome. Now I must go to the ward. I look forward to both of you visiting ICU this afternoon."

"Yes. Goodbye for now, Dr. Wei."

"Goodbye, Miss Merry Ann."

Really, it wasn't magic as I thought then. Dr. Wei must have decided to open the door for us. He saw something in us that was worth allowing in. To every part of the hospital. Tongsi with everyone. Such fun Nurse Lai and I had, delving into all the nooks and crannies of that hospital. The traditional pharmacists invited us to open the narrow wooden drawers to discover dried herbs, fungii and roots. "Come back! Come back for good medicine!" they called. Up we climbed to the eagle's nest, the Art Department, that made technical slides, and paintings of panda bears for the waiting rooms. In the hallway behind Emergency sat a row of patients puffing into the mouthpieces of steam machines. Up on the wards, families camped on the bed of their patient, feeding and bathing them. Some watched in quiet vigilance, others talked with their neighbours and called out to the nurses who flitted in and out with meds.

One afternoon we strayed down a back corridor, to a sign that translated to Electrical Therapy. What's this? A branch of Chinese Physio? That's when I had the good luck to meet Yuen. Right away we became attached to each other, and whenever I had space in my schedule, we worked with patients together. She listened to my explanations of movement therapy through Nurse Lai's translation. Then she would describe her approach at equal length for me. I watched Yuen for the subtle changes in her strong expressive face, her direct, almost confronting glances at me, and her strong voice, speaking truth. She stood in her white lab coat with legs apart, arms down, not moving, as she spoke. She moved with purpose, never in excess. One day, after we had tried each other's techniques with a taxi driver's neck pain, she took me by the shoulders, and smiled at me with all her features. I was with her in this, a true comrade. It was direct, between us. Conrad wasn't there, to dilute it with his expert systems. Isn't that a mean thing to say? It was something I got to have for myself, a wise woman beside me.

Conrad's work was so impressive, and I couldn't help thinking of myself as an add-on. That's a very poor habit, thinking of myself that way. I wonder where it comes from? Nothing obvious. Still, it's hard to change our ways of thinking. Even Conrad has trouble with that. Wouldn't it be interesting if some Chinese ways rubbed off on him?

We developed a way of offering the most we could in the short time we had: Conrad giving the lectures, presenting the written explanations, while I demonstrated on staff or patients. Conrad was determined to pour his expertise into the Chinese system, to bring it up to the right standard. We were quite an entourage: Nurse Lai and a crowd of doctors and nurses gathered at the bedside, while parents, aunts and uncles perched around the bed. We had to get it all done by four o'clock because the meal carts came along with their steaming cauldrons. Families got fed too. Most of them seemed to sleep at the bedside, on a chair or end of the bed, or on a mat on the floor. No wonder the sick person, especially the kids, seemed so calm, with that support 24 hours a day.

There's a wonderful rhythm we got into, working day after day together, talking about how it went, at lunch and supper in the tiny dining room, then planning for the next day and writing up notes for staff in the evening. Nurse Lai had a hoarse throat and writer's cramp from all we asked her to do. What a treasure! Every minute, she was enthusiastic.

She reminded me of my Sweet Emily. So I wrote to her, explaining how Nurse Lai was like my daughter in a home away from home:

> ... and I've never felt more peaceful, looked after and safe in our cocoon, the hospital. It's so clear what we have to do. Everyone supports us. We have a wonderful colleague (tongsi) named Dr. Wei. I feel we belong, though Conrad keeps his professional distance better than me. If we don't look in the mirror we can imagine that we are part of China.
>
> Now that Nurse Lai is more fluent in English, she confides in me all about her family, especially her mother who restricts her more than she would like (even though she is married.) It sounds just like you and me! I told her about your prom dress, the limo and corsage. She was quite amazed. That's fancier than her wedding. She showed me a photo of their banquet at a hotel by the river. She and her husband took me on a karaoke boat one evening. All Chinese pop songs, except one that I could join in on – "Yesterday". Everyone loves singing. Maybe it's freedom of a sort. After a banquet for some bigwigs from Beijing, the guests stood up and began a rousing military-

sounding song. Then they insisted that Conrad and I sing! So we dredged up some tunes from the old London days, and favourites like "Loch Lomond." They joined in and at the end we crossed hands and sang "Auld Lang Syne." Conrad's face was quite glowing. Wouldn't Daddy be amazed to see his wife doing something like this?

He would be so proud of you, sweetie—your great marks in school, and looking after Hans and Connie. You wrote that you're feeling some pressure with everything. I know it's so tricky, but you're very wise to cool things off with Chris for a bit. It'd be so easy to get distracted, with him not being in school. Tell Grandma not to worry about arranging Connie's swimming lessons. I'll do it when I get back. If Hans is having so much trouble with math, I'm sure Mr. Simpson next door would go over it with him. Good luck in your exams. And don't forget what a peach you are to give Grandma so much help. Tons of hugs to you all.

Love, Mum"

I think Nurse Lai understood what Conrad still meant to me. Early in December I asked her to help me make a special request to Mrs. Wong. Could the hospital cooks prepare a particular dish instead of the routine repertoire that always came our way?

"It's made with beef or fish and eggplant. There's a stall on Renmin Road that makes it."

"Is it hot pot? Spicy? Sauce brown and juicy? Yu Hun Keh Tzi Boh?"

"Yes, that's it! It's Conrad's favourite dish. I want to surprise him on his birthday."

Nurse Lai winked and smiled in her puckish way. She spoke to Mrs. Wong with her darting hands and smiles and persuading quick voice. Mrs. Wong looked doubtful, then interested, and finally won over. She bowed and creased her whole face and turned toward the kitchen in that small-step, shuffling-slipper way of older Chinese ladies.

The next day, sure enough, Yu Hun Keh Tzi Boh arrived.

"Conrad, this is your birthday dinner! Happy Birthday!"

It wasn't often that I saw his composure slip. He even blushed. And I began to serve him. It was so hot, the steam rose from his plate. He looked over the little table, filled with simple enamel dishes, white pot of tea, plain bowls chipped here and there. He gave me one of those rare dazzling smiles of long ago.

"Marian, I didn't think you'd still remember. No one else has."

"Oh, the mail is awfully slow." Something made me reach out my hand to his, like the old days. "Con, you know I still love you. Even after all this time."

And then something I thought I'd never see: tears, spilled from his eyes. He looked down and said so quietly I almost didn't hear, "You're the only woman in my life now. You're precious to me too."

Oh Con.

We heard running steps in the hall and Nurse Lai came bursting in with her eager smile, carrying a little basket with a red bow tied around the handle. Lychees and star fruits peeked out. "Dr. Conrad! Please have Chinese fruits for Happy Birthday! Good Health! Long Life!"

He just had time to say, "Doh Jeh!" and off she ran.

We laughed. We could be carefree again, but with that glow of love that old friends share, who've been through thick and thin together.

I guess we kind of formed the Conrad-and-Marian team, in those months. But we didn't realize how fragile it was.

On the weekends we began cooking our own versions of the new dishes we'd been tasting. Nurse Lai taught us the key words so we could buy fresh produce from the street vendors. One Saturday evening we cooked up quite a feast on the hotplate in the centre of our blue tile counter: soup with lotus root and mushrooms, rice, bean curd with greens, and some succulent shrimps. We toasted each other with tea: Buon Appetito! like the old days at Mario's. While we did the dishes we regaled ourselves with favourite songs from the flat in London. Instead of settling down to his reports as usual, I was surprised to watch Con rummaging in the glass bookcase in the corner next to the donated Japanese tapedeck. He flipped through the tapes.

"Well, what have we got here? Polish Polka Party? Not tonight… People's Fourth Urology Congress? No thanks… Eine Kleine Nachtmusich? Another time… Tango Fiesta? Perfect!"

And just like that, we whisked ourselves back to the dance clubs of London. "Marian! You haven't forgotten!" He smiled down at me.

"You taught me well, Con."

How could I forget what it was like to be held by him, a young girl fresh off the boat? The pause and the turn, the legs interleaved, the slow and the quick, the promise of more.

He guided me past the windows, past Neurology Ward 3 across the lane, where nurses were preparing their patients for the night. But we didn't notice. We were immersed in that special rhythm of the tango. We turned and our eyes chanced to meet.

His eyes were so close that I could see the golden flecks again. We paused and he leaned slightly forward. A shock went through me, the recognition of desire. I'd have died and gone to heaven if he'd really meant it – before. But now? Beautiful as he was, perfect in every way, his closeness suddenly seemed wrong. Why?

I'm a girl no longer. I'm a woman with three children: a widow and the head of my family. I've been through the wars: had cancer, been disfigured and survived. And he's a mature man with a male partner. The old days of romance, the fantasy that never was, is not reality now either. I don't belong to you any more, Conrad Falk.

I jumped back. I'm afraid I was cruelly tactless: "No! It's no good!"

The shock and pain on his face said it all. I ran from my destruction into my bedroom.

At breakfast, I tried to mend what I had done. "Conrad, about last night...I'm..."

"No. Just leave it."

So. That was that.

Conrad's skill at formal discretion smoothed over the first frigid week of working and eating together. In the evenings, his report writing became more detailed and absorbing, while I wrote more letters home. I wish I could have explained it to him. I should have apologized to him. After a while his silence convinced me that my rejection didn't matter. It was just a moment of misunderstanding. I had the illusion that we could almost return to what we had before. It was a relief to be with our tongsi, who helped fill the empty space between us. He increased his commitment to the post-surgical ward, extending his expertise and dedication to long hours of on-call, as he did at the Royal. His work was never finished. Everyone admired him so much. I learned to explore the neighbourhood around the hospital by myself. Then Dr. Wei invited me to go with him to the park.

Maybe he felt I might be lonely on Sundays, not having anything to do. It was so thoughtful, considering all he had on his plate. I would've been fine, on my own, but you can't turn down someone's hospitality. Was it a way of passing back the hosting that he received during his study tour of Canada? I'll have to remember that: to spread the kindness outward, like ripples when a stone is thrown into the lake.

One Friday when I was taking off my isolation gown outside the door of ICU, Dr. Wei came up the stairs on his way in.

"Good morning."

"Good morning, Dr. Wei. It's good to see Baby Wu is getting better."

He smiled, folding his thin arms around his lab coat. "Yes, he's out of the woods, as you say. Miss Merry Ann, I've been meaning to ask you, there is a garden I'd like you to see. Would you be free on Sunday to go there?"

I couldn't help laughing. "Dr. Wei, I'm always free!"

"Well, that's good. I'll meet you in the hospital entrance by the bicycle racks. Would 2 o'clock be all right?"

"Yes, that would be lovely."

"Good. Now, did you have a chance to show Nurse Fong the postural drainage positions?"

On Sunday, he was waiting for me, sure enough. Instead of the rumpled lab coat, he was wearing "civvies": that green and black windbreaker, and a white shirt and tie. The collar was several sizes too large, so the structure of his thin neck was exposed, like the detailed drawing in *Grant's Atlas of Anatomy*. His brown pants, street market variety, were a little too short, which revealed his black leather shoes, slim and polished.

"Nei ho ma, Dr. Wei."

"Good afternoon, Miss Merry Ann."

He stepped toward the street and raised his hand to hail a taxi, but I ran over and touched his sleeve. "Dr. Wei, could we take the bus?"

Just for an instant, he looked horrified. "A foreign guest shouldn't be taking the bus."

"Oh, I'd really like to. I haven't had a chance yet."

He looked quite dubious, even embarrassed, then smiled. "As you wish, Miss Merry Ann."

So we jumped on the 103 bus up Renmin Road to the West Garden. Even on Sunday the traffic roared along the West Road. It was a longish walk past the birdmarket, with the most gorgeous coloured birds stacked in cages, a few still cheeping but most hunched with heads down, waiting. Small boys played with tiny lizards under the trees while their fathers played chess. As we entered the moon gate, a green waft of cool air greeted us. Trees with thick roped trunks and huge branches with broad leaves sheltered the path. We crunched along on the gravel underfoot.

"This is my favourite garden. Not many people come here."

"Have you always lived in Guangzhou?"

"I was born in Guilin. After my training I came here. I was stationed far away for many years."

"Why was that? Or should I not ask?"

His smile was so gentle, his cheek bones stood out, and his black eyes watched me from deep in his face. I was aware of the bones around his eyes; he was so thin. Spare and kind. "Yes, I am happy to tell you. It was very common. Young people of my generation were sent away to work."

"Was it part of growing up?"

"In a way. It was in the time of the Cultural Revolution. At that time city children were sent to the country to learn hard labour."

"That must have been terrible, to leave your family. How old were you?"

"About 15. It was not all terrible. But I was very hungry. The farmers didn't really want the city children; they didn't want to have to teach us how to work. But it was the orders. We had to grow our food, but we weren't good at it."

"Where was this?"

"In the West, some distance from Chengdu. In the mountains, it got very cold. We had to learn ways to keep warm, such as lying with the animals."

I thought about that. I knew there was a lot he wasn't telling me. I couldn't bear to ask for more details. "You must have learned a lot about endurance."

"Oh, yes. And I made some wonderful friends. We still get together, for Dim Sum. We love to eat together! Many of us live in Guangzhou now."

"Your experiences then, is that one of the reasons that you can work so hard? You always seem to be at work, early and late."

He was smiling at me again. Was I such a naive Westerner? A gauche woman?

"Yes. We Chinese people know how to work hard. But it is a matter of Qi."

"Qi?"

"Yes. Qi is vitality. It is universal energy. It is everywhere."

An odd sensation took hold of me; a quickening. Here was something I needed to know about.

"Please tell me about Qi."

"All right. But first let's have tea. It's a tradition to sit in the teahouse in a garden, and converse while we enjoy tea."

So we entered a pavilion with open sides, with a few tables around the edge, and couples quietly talking. In one corner an elderly woman in plain grey Mao suit was playing an extraordinary stringed instrument. A breeze came in from the garden, and an occasional butterfly. An attendant brought a big pot and plain white cups. In his precise way, Dr. Wei poured the strong black tea with floating sticks and leaves and began talking, his eyes gazing at the garden outside.

"Qi is the fire of vitality, and also the coolness and peace of vitality. It is the balance of the flow of Qi that brings well-being. In the West, medicine has quick fixes of dramatic result. But to build up the Qi, to sustain our lives, is a gradual process. In little children, there is strong Qi. A child comes "trailing clouds of glory," as your poet says. The cup, given to him by his parents, is full of the purity, freshness, and strength of his ancestry.

In the West, there is the delusion that vitality will be strengthened by external products that are provocatively advertised. It is the same with medicine. People in the West (and the East too) want the doctor to provide them with a cure from outside themselves. They receive technically advanced testing, prescriptions, and surgical procedures. But the balance of energy, neither excess nor depletion, is ignored.

When I arrived to study medicine in Toronto, living as a foreigner was very complicated and confusing. I thought I had already learned English, but I was far from understanding the underlying meaning behind the words. Despite the great personal freedom that I had heard about, people were often constrained from speaking what they really thought. At hospital meetings, some people pushed ahead too quickly with their own "mandate" and "agenda," disregarding the harmony required for satisfactory decision-making. Many women looked angry, fighting to get into powerful positions. There were subtle undercurrents that rivalled the ancient mandarin bureaucracy. In the competitive atmosphere and personal isolation I perceived a great dissipation of Qi."

"It must have been lonely for you, Dr. Wei." He regarded me for a second, then examined the bottom of his teacup. Oh, have I stepped too close? But no, it's okay.

"Yes, at first it was difficult to be parted from my wife. At that time she wanted a child very much. We have learned to delay our happiness but keep our hope. Toronto was very strange to me at first. There were so few people walking around. Not like Guangzhou! And no familiar sounds, only the sound of cars. But my colleagues were very kind. They showed me many new things: camping, and sailing, and Niagara Falls. And I could read books about China that I can't read here. That freedom was worth more to me than all the meals in restaurants and other luxuries. On my return, I left my clothes behind, and filled my suitcases with books."

I laughed, but then realized how poignant this was. "Chinese people seem to know how to bear a great deal. Perhaps you are more disciplined and restrained than Westerners."

He took off his glasses, polished them on his jacket sleeve, and carefully replaced them. Two herons on a small island out in the green pond, clacking and flapping their wings around their nest, caught his attention for a moment. I refilled his teacup. He turned toward me again.

"Yes, I suppose that is true. We are more modest. We don't display our bodies in public. We don't hug and kiss people we have only just met. Even shaking hands takes getting used to, especially between a man and a woman. We don't call strangers by their first name. In China, first names are reserved for very close friends. But that doesn't mean that we don't have the same passions. I'm sure you have heard about the extremes of our behaviour."

(Extremes, meaning hatred and crime? War? Have you experienced that, Dr. Wei?) We paused to watch the herons fly over the avenue of trees at the edge of the park, out over the city. He continued.

"Beauty is a great antidote to suffering. All the beauty in the world carries elements of Qi. It is said that just as night is gradually followed by day, and day is followed by night, the vital energies fluctuate in the world and find expression. The flow of contrasts is very satisfying to observe, and can be supported. We need to strengthen our Qi, as it is depleted by the damaging aspects of our lives. And we can help each other. Do you see that little boy, running with his kite on the grass? Long ago, my father took me kite-flying. Perhaps one day I will watch my son fly his kite in this park. The child supports our vitality as we watch him play. When my wife cooks a meal with foods that complement each other, and is beautifully prepared, our Qi is enhanced. Even in the rubble of demolished buildings, the people can have smoothly flowing Qi if they are in harmony together. And there are deeper and more fleeting expressions of Qi known to the wise. Do you understand?"

"I'm wondering if it's what the flamenco dancers talk about, the Duende."

"I don't know that word, Miss Merry Ann. What does it mean?"

"I think it has something to do with strength coming out of suffering. One time I danced with some gypsies in Spain and watched them performing. Since ancient times they have been pushed to the edge of society so they sing about loneliness and persecution and the passion to survive. The guitarist gives a distinctive rhythm for the dancers. The people watching usually clap and call out, to support them. The postures express pride, even defiance. You can see the tension and strong contrast between male and female, but also celebration. The pace gathers momentum or slows to a pause. It's dark and bright like glowing fire. I could feel myself being pulled toward the spirit of the dancers and afterward feeling elated, almost mesmerized."

"There is no doubt that you are talking about the building of Qi." We paused and thought about this. He looked straight at me then, as a doctor would. "Miss Merry Ann, would you permit me to take your pulse?" I extended my hand to him. "I feel many things in your pulse. Your circulation of energy is currently quite low. The strength that you have to call upon is tentative. You have come to help and support us. You have been wounded during your life, like all of us. But deep in you is a joyful person full of Qi. While you are here, we will give you what you need to help us and sustain you so that when you go back to your country, you will be strengthened, not weakened, from your time here."

I was touched. "Thank you, Dr. Wei. You are right. I have had cancer, and I still fear for my life. I had my breast removed and I have to trust that chemotherapy and radiation killed the cancer cells and now I can start again. Sometimes I feel terrified about having a recurrence, and I just don't know what to do about it. Nobody can tell me that, I guess. I just have to figure it out myself. Don't I?"

"Miss Merry Ann, do you see that pink and white peony, beside the path? It is called, "Xin Shi Qi Hua", meaning, 'Special in the World'. That is you."

I couldn't find a word to respond to that. He went on. "Many things you already know how to do. And there are many things I can offer you, such as herbs and exercises and acupuncture. You can build your Qi. You will teach me Western Rehabilitation and I will teach you Eastern Rehabilitation. Then we will both be strong! ... Ah, I find it so relaxing, having tea here, with the breezes coming through the teahouse and the serene colour of the algae on the pond. Do you hear that delicate melody being played on the Cheng? It is called 'Wild Geese Descend On Level Sands.'"

We listened suspended in that ancient music, in that ancient place. Then he spoke, very quietly. "The hospital seems far away, but it is waiting. Perhaps we'll come again another day?"

"Do you come here with your wife? Does she work near the Hospital?"

"No, she works in Shanghai. Her business keeps her for long, long hours, and she seldom comes home. We are used to being apart. One day you will meet her."

"Would she mind, that I sit with you and have tea?"

Now there was a question. At first Dr. Wei averted his eyes and his expression became more remote and formal. But then he turned his warm dark gaze on me and bowed ever so slightly. "Do not worry. It is possible to have a close friendship without being disloyal. I think that is true. Do you?"

"Yes, it is very possible."

It must have been several weeks later, after our visit to the West Garden, that I dreamed of Conrad encased in ice. There was no colour in him — he was rigid, white and grey. I pounded and pounded on the ice with my fists. I kicked and kicked, then threw my body against that block, but his mask face remained unchanged inside. A horrible fear began to pervade me: feeling my colour bleeding away, feeling myself chilling into immobile silence. Caught again in the fear of silence, the fear of unnamed death. I woke up, my pink quilt fallen rumpled on the floor, and as I reached down to pull it round me, a cockroach dropped out of it and scuttled for cover under the bed.

I lay there waiting for my breathing to slow down. There was sharp pain in my ribs. I poked around, finding a few tender places down and to the right of my scar. The day's work distracted me but the next morning it was the same, and of course I thought it was cancer returning. The chance of living to be a little old lady goes way down if the original breast cancer wanders off somewhere else. I couldn't keep the panic down with sensible logic. The vision of Michelle grey with pain in her bones and everywhere wouldn't be pushed away. Was this something I would have to deal with by myself in China? How?

I decided to ask Conrad. How could I do that, after the rift between us? How I wished for those old innocent days, when we knew how to care for each other! Before the layers of sophistication veiled what we really felt. Before hurts piled up, one upon another. If those days really had existed. Yes, we knew how to extend our hands to each other then. I had to hope that warm love was still there, though buried. I needed someone, and I thought it was him. I spoke to him as casually as I could, after breakfast.

"Oh, Conrad. I've had some aching. It's quite persistent." His face looked stern, cool and clinical. His eyes were different now, almost grey, instead of gold.

"It's probably muscular. Where's the pain?"

I thought, "Maybe this is a mistake. He seems so cold, like my dream. He doesn't care. I can't reveal my body to him. No man has looked at me since Josef, and of course Dr. Lorenzini. Anyway, my body's ugly now. What disgust would Conrad politely conceal?"

I kept things simple. "In my chest. Maybe my ribs."

"Near your mastectomy site?"

"Yes. I think so."

"You've probably strained yourself from lifting the kids every day."

"Yeah, that's probably it. I'll just forget it." Fat chance.

"Get a chest xray done. If there's anything to worry about, that'll show it up."

Yes, logical and sensible. Underneath, did he feel any of my panic? There didn't seem any point in going on about it. Oh no. "Good idea."

No words in any language can describe the pit of fear that overwhelmed me then. I was incapable of pushing the spectre of cancer away. It wasn't a visual form; it was invisible. And silent. Inside me, and with the greatest stealth, so I wouldn't notice, it was seeping into and poisoning the life that was me. The worst part was that the cancer was me, of my own making. It was more intimate than even my thoughts. I couldn't call it an enemy because it was part of myself. I couldn't keep the sense of shame from soaking into me, or the longing to hide, to be private about this terrible failure in myself. I couldn't expose myself to Chinese scrutiny. I didn't want to go out into the open, march downstairs to Xray, take off my shirt and say, "Here I am, Exhibit A."

Finally Dr. Wei took me aside after Neuro Rounds, and quietly said, "Forgive me for asking, Miss Merry Ann, but is there something wrong? Are you ill?"

I didn't know what to say. "I'm not sure. Maybe it's nothing."

He led me gently to the meds room behind the ward office where the staff write and study reports. "If you like, please tell me about this."

"Dr. Wei, I have these painful spots between my ribs. Maybe the radiation didn't get all the cancer. I feel sure that it's spread to my ribs and it's eating its way into my liver and maybe my brain. Maybe my body is beginning to crumble."

I began to shake. He sat me down in a wooden chair and placed his hands on my shoulders. He remained standing over me, saying nothing and after a while I let out some more. "What's to become of my children if I die soon? ...They're too young yet. It's so stupid, that I can't even stay alive for my children! Eating myself up! This creeping silly cancer... how can I outwit it? ...Dr. Wei, do you know how?"

By the strength of his hands on my shoulders he stood me up and surrounded me with his thin arms. At last I could give in. My head fell on his bony shoulder and I sank limp into him at last. All the sobbing I had saved up for years, about everything, including Conrad, flooded away. I felt like I had fallen to the bottom of the sea and he was the cave that I could slip into like an octopus, that needed quiet safe darkness. I emptied myself into him.

He led me away down a hall, and up some stairs. "Miss Merry Ann, I will be your doctor. First I'll examine you. Then we'll take some pictures. Nurse Fong, help Miss Merry Ann with her clothes."

He asked me gentle questions – what hurts and where. He examined me both sides. They took some blood for testing. Someone took xrays in a small back room. Then I sat on the plinth and waited.

I looked down at myself. I realized I was thinner now. My two sides were so different. The roundness on the left side plummeted to the rocky shore of the right: the cliffs of sternum and ribs, the exaggerated promontory of shoulder. But I wasn't ashamed – it was just me. I tied the hospital gown around my neck again.

Dr. Wei came back. And smiled. He didn't tell me what was going on with me or what I should do. He asked me. Now that's strange. Up until then, I'd had rules and people knowing what's best for me. With advice and kind sympathy. Stern warnings too, and experts knowing the answers and looking at me with the eyes of technology. He asked me what I thought about myself now. So I told him, tentatively at first.

"My xray is normal, I think."

"Yes, it is."

"The pain is in the intercostal muscles, not the bones."

"Yes."

"My blood is quite balanced and there are no indications of cancer."

"Yes, you are right."

"And I am still beautiful."

"Yes, there's no doubt."

And then we looked at each other with mischievous eyes, and laughed. We laughed! If we'd had champagne on the cart by the plinth, we'd have drunk till we were tipsy. I probably would have taught Dr. Wei some high school jive steps – who knows? Instead, he prescribed those herbs for me, from Traditional Pharmacy, to build my immune system gradually over time: the thin root, the wide root, the red seeds, a fungus, and dried leaves, boiled together.

That day I stopped thinking of cancer with a paralyzing fear. My life became an improvised dance instead. Directed by me. I began the process of healing, of learning to sustain myself, though there's been a certain amount of back-sliding, I must admit.

Ventilation and Perfusion. Positioning and Vibration. Cardiac Monitoring and Oxygen Saturation. Mobilizing and Stasis. The working words that define Conrad's world. Translations of what we patients feel. Signposts on the road we've both travelled. But I'm not listening to that message any more. I'm learning a different language now. Balance and Patience. Anxiety and Hope. Qi and Meridians. Yin and Yang. New signs keep cropping up on my road. Even then it was getting harder to recognize him. Was the face of my first beloved turning to stone and leaching away? Or did I just not see him with the same eyes as before?

At a reception for the visiting Minister of Health, Dr. Cheng, Vice-Director of Outpatient Services, told me about the special places in China, that are revered historically. One of them is Guilin, where she said the painters have gathered to rhapsodize on the classical mountain landscape. Unique-shaped mountains rise from the plain, the rice-fields, and beside the River Li. They are repeated variations on the tumulus of mysterious geological remains, knees and elbows poking up from the earth. They recede in misty watery greys, framed in silk in the galleries, and in the camera lenses of the new tourists. It is a special place because of the caves and the war. The delicate arrangements that allowed me to visit Dr. Wei's birthplace awoke Conrad's suspicions. But why?

"I can't see any need for you to spread the word up there. Our mandate is to demonstrate a solid programme in one place. Guangzhou."

"But Dr. Wei's gone to a lot of trouble. His colleagues at the university want to hear about community-based rehab. It's only for a few days."

"Oh well, do what you want."

Hmm. Dr. Wei made up a small delegation. Two other tongsi travelled with us, the resident in the premature nursery and the junior member of the Traditional Chinese Medicine department. The doctors in the hospital at Guilin University brought in some infants and young children with cerebral palsy, for physiotherapy assessment and treatment demonstration.

We gathered in the austere meeting room, the staff seated in straight chairs in neat rows before my improvised treatment space with mat, roll and large ball. Dr. Wei translated my introduction. Then the first baby, Chi Chai, was brought to my mat by her mother. She was a little nervous with me, a scary foreigner, but we smiled and together unwrapped some of her clothes and blankets. Because the baby was a severe spastic, she could barely move, and in abnormal patterns. I cradled her and stroked her, curled up so she felt safe. Beneath her smooth baby skin her tight muscles were governed by primitive reflexes, distorted by her pathology. I had a few moments to hold this life and use my knowledge through my hands to convey what my system could do for this child. The white-coated audience leaned forward to watch my every move, but I had no magic to give them, only an alternative to the techniques they already practised on their children.

I began moving Chi Chai in the alert and wordless state of my experience as a therapist, in that place where time is lost in the present moment...

My hands hold her and shift her and roll her to observe how she responds. Her flow of developmental time is stuttering and flawed. The progression through evolution that Mrs. Bobath taught me is the brain's message for every baby, that stays with us in our movement all through our lives, is my guide to what I observe. My perception is only partly conscious but I trust it to understand how to move with Chi Chai. Together we explore how the worms slithered through the ancient ooze. We grope with the fishes through the caverned depths of the sea. We grasp with our toes in an amphibian hold on the lumpiness of earth still muddy from the flood. We creep with the hairy whiskered quadrupeds under the sunlit canopy of leaves. We rise up with the giant hunters to meet the clouds swirling around the thrusting cliffs. This tiny girl teaches me the history inside myself, as I try to draw out her humanity. It is a child's game full of mischievous surprise, as well as of solemn reverence. Chi Chai laughs...

The laugh ripples outwards: who can resist a little kid chuckling? I am humming a nursery rhyme, and a white-haired woman in the front row begins singing some Chinese words. Dr.

Wei whispers, "It's a grandmother's song." In a moment of effortless flexibility, the baby turns her head and with a questing stretch of her fingers, reaches for her mother. Language and time are unimportant as we sit watching the expression of this little person's life, freed in a small way from the trap that holds her. Chi Chai is teaching me how to free myself. She makes it possible to feel the warmth of these people who I cannot even speak to. They are giving strength to me, just as much as I am giving strength to her...

I gave the child back to her mother, and we smiled as partners. After more demonstrations, and some translated discussion, Dr. Wei and I shook hands with everyone, and said goodbye. We took the bus through the busy shopping district, away from the university, to the outskirts, where there were many more trees. All the way I thought about little Chi Chai and how Dr. Wei had arranged the day.

We walked quite a way from the last bus stop, and came to the rice fields, along a road edged with flowering bushes somewhat like pink rhododendrons. Trucks with slatted and canvas canopies rumbled by, with many people, men and women, standing up and leaning over in the back.

"Where are they going, Dr. Wei?"

"There's a factory over there. Some are soldiers. Those places have been here since the war."

He seemed guarded, rather closed off. I was entering the territory of his history.

To the left of the road were rice fields with farmers bending over in their cone-shaped hats that reminded me of the spruce root hats of the Haida people. A water buffalo and man ploughed one watery field that reflected the famous-shaped mountains beyond. Nearby another farmer and motorized plough growled through the mud. The skyline of Guilin in the west looked like a mirage, especially as piling clouds advanced, shot with crackles of lightning.

"A storm is coming. We'll find a cave near here to wait it out."

On the knobbly mountain ahead, a black circle like a mouth opened to us. He led the way, climbing the steep rock face until we were inside. It was only a tiny recess, with the ashes of a campfire at the back, near the blackened cave wall.

"I came here as a child. I have watched many storms from here."

The clouds were dark and looming over us. Thunder banged around. The rice farmers finally gave up, as sheets of rain beat down. All the world was pale grey. They trudged away bent down, with their machine and water buffalo, picking their way along the grassy edge between water-soaked fields.

"There are so many caves in these mountains. My father and his group could hide from the Japanese and store ammunition for the Communist cause."

"Was he a guerrilla fighter then?"

"Fighting for freedom for the people. His goal was to relieve their suffering and create a better life for all of us."

Dr. Wei sat on his heels like a hunched heron.

"You must be proud of him," I said after awhile, he was so quiet.

"He gave his life for us. Now it is my responsibility to continue his life's work, in my own way. I must never stop this effort."

I was struck silent by his idealism. He had been stamped by his history.

We looked out together at the outline of the city, now sparkling with sunshine reflections on the glass of apartment blocks, and at the empty rice fields that had been worked for hundreds of years. There, change and eternity co-exist. I sat waiting for memories to wash through him. I was a witness to something I knew nothing of. At last he stood up and turned to the west, to watch the sun casting extravagant beams in our direction, playing prism with the rain droplets. A white fog rose like breath from the rice fields. Without speaking, he led the way down again. We slowly returned to the bus stop.

On the bus, Dr. Wei patiently sat with calm face, to let his feeling ebb back to the normal day. At last he turned toward me, and did a rare thing. He placed his hand on top of mine. "Chinese people have a long history. We learn to endure many things. Thank you for your friendship."

Dr. Wei. What did your father feel when he stared into the cave at the bear of death? Or was it a dragon? Courage, I think. And you stare at it too. Now I can recall, whenever I need it, like right now, in this desert, the warmth and strength of you that will help me to endure.

Lying on this earth with the sun pushing away the darkness, I can envision you speaking softly to me, "When you are breathing in, my arms are holding you. When you are breathing out, my mind encircles you. When you are breathing in, my hand is stroking you. When you are breathing out, my heart enfolds you."

I am resting, waiting for the new day.

The next morning Dr. Wei attended ward rounds with his tongsi and then we boarded the bus for a day trip to the famous River Li. In Yangshuo we rented bikes and loaded them on a small, low boat held by a grizzled boatman. He steered out into the smooth-flowing river, past the famous knobbly mountains and feathery bamboo lining the shore. A teal-blue and lime-green landscape. Occasionally, water birds flew up before us, maybe cranes or storks, and then around a bend, was the vision of a village just like those in the paintings, with old wooden houses and a steeply-curving pagoda by a flight of stone steps. The boatman dropped us off, unloaded our bikes, and headed away along the river. His bamboo fishing rod bowed to us until he was lost in the watery haze.

Dr. Wei led me up the steps to sit in the small pavilion, and took from his bicycle bag a pomelo. With his pocket knife he cut away the thick skin, in precise slices. I watched his fingers, thin and dextrous like the rest of him. The fruit was sweet and pithy. I looked into the water, pale with no reflection or white frilly waves: a milky skin. I longed to slip under its surface.

"Dr. Wei, would it be alright if I go for a swim?"

A tiny smile escaped him. "Yes, there are no dragons."

So I shed my green pants and jacket. I had on a thick T-shirt and underwear modest enough, not to embarrass Dr. Wei. I slowly slipped into the River Li. Circles spread out from my arms, over and over. I watched the surface of the river ahead, then I looked down and into the milky green. Shafts of light fingered through the top, but deep down the green darkened. My hair was free. My head was delightfully cool. My body seemed to be softening. And my mind was released at last. No language or any human contact could hinder my sense of myself. A self of layers, back through time. A self as fluid as water. Up to the surface again, and around to look at the shore. Dr. Wei sat in the shadow of the pavilion with its blue roof tiles curling up at the corners. He looked like a poet in an old fashioned scroll painting, the glint of his pocket knife in his hand like a brush.

Under the surface again, the sunlight came down in columns until it dissipated into the deep green. Other waves of light ran from the depths into the shore, always in that direction. Disks of light played with each other, circles hiding and re-appearing, silvery quick. Strong lines of light crisscrossed each other in wavy diamonds. I found that by crisscrossing my limbs like the light, I could twist my whole body in the water. My hands wanted to twist too, like a dancer, as my head and trunk arced right and then left. My arms wanted to twist in alternating waves, but my legs wanted to step, with toes pointed, in spreading strides. My trunk and pelvis began curving and arcing until my entire body was twisting, like a dogfish…

    I am the dogfish that dreams, and swims alone. I glide grey and white in a plane of my seven senses. This space of rippled green is all my world. My nose thrusts forward as my body waves side to side in a smooth curve. I am aware of males pursuing me, swimming behind and beside and beneath me. One darts forward and grabs my left pectoral fin. I twist upward and roll so my white underside captures the light from above. I flip my tail to struggle away but the male hangs on, clamping my fin with his teeth. I writhe down in rolling loops to the sandy floor and the male twines around me. We are linked, our tubular silver and steel bodies splashed with stars. We pause and twist again. Then his length swings outward from his grasp on my fin. With a powerful urge, I roll and flick my tail, releasing myself from his teeth. I swim long and smooth and fast and away from capture, into a fissure in the undersea rocks. A place of shallow water opens around me and I glide for a long time. Bands of light and green weed wave over the white sand. Small lives are struggling to leave my body. My tail sweeps from side to side over and over and I circle over the sand while my baby slips out and wriggles away. And another. And another, the last one. I sense them nearby, smooth and glowing like me. At last I swim away from them and rest on the sandy bottom until the darkness comes. My five gill slits open and close and my fins and tail flash me into darting action. With the ampullae on my cheeks, that sense without sight or sound, the special perception of my species, I search for delicious fish. I satiate myself with my jagged halfmoon mouth. I am strong and beautiful...

I rise to the surface. Now I roll only my centre and leave my limbs to follow, like seaweed. I turn and turn and watch the riverscape swing in a circle, the pagoda and shore of bamboo fronds, the blueness of undulating land and sky, while my body dances under the surface. Submerging again in body and mind, I feel my head swelling, my eyes beginning to bulge, my nose becoming less tapered, more rounded. I have a long tongue now. My skin loses its toughness, becoming softer and more pliable. I feel the greenness of the water soaking into me. My spinal column is tingling with messages, my flanks become charged with exquisite tiny energies. The memory of my breast, that was removed, my right one, is glowing and part of me like an ancestral bud. Both breasts are light and inconsequential for this new life. My legs spread out – they want to be more active – they uncurl in a spring and take large strides. Now I have long toes and fingers. My arms reach outward too and turn and flex and extend in a leaping rhythm. As I swim down and down I realise I am green like the water and blowing bubbles through my round mouth now. Some weeds waving on their slender stalks beckon to me. I swim among them into the shallow water. Deep in my centre, in my core, I feel very warm, though the water and my limbs feel cool. Now the land beckons and I swim in a straight line, limbs spreading apart and closing together, frog-like, until I reach the steps. I climb slowly, dripping water, until I reach the stone seat. Only the pomelo skin is still there, its white pith exposed and drying in the sun. Dr. Wei has disappeared. I turn my face to the sun and feel the green slipping away. There is such a pleasure now in being warm and dry. Glancing around, I notice the brilliance of all the colours. The old cracked timbers of the pavilion are carved and painted red, green and black. Some iridescent birds resembling swallows dart across the water. Rustling jade-green fronds of bamboo wave by the bank. It's a familiar strong feeling to be back on land again...

Reaching for my jacket and pants that were warmed by the sun, I dressed again. I felt new, like the person I used to be before I left Herring Cove or knew about the world. But changed from that. Old and new at the same time.

I followed the steep path into FuLi and found Dr. Wei in a dark shop, chatting with a painter and examining long panels of rice paper, traditional-style ink studies. They greeted me pleasantly and carried on with their discussion, as if this was a normal day. The painter's grey hair stood up in bristles on his head, and his eyebrows were thick and black like brushstrokes. He handed me a scroll on which he had painted two birds that I took to be pheasants. They curved around each other in a dramatic circle. One's tail was longer and straight, the other a waving arc.

Dr. Wei explained, "This is Feng-Huang, Miss Merry Ann, the Supreme Yang and the Supreme Yin. Western people call it Phoenix. This is for you." Such a gift I will never receive again.

We walked back to our bikes. We looked over the handlebars at each other and smiled. I couldn't help wondering how much Dr. Wei understood about what had happened inside me. We bicycled through the village, past the old wooden houses, the market square, the field where a water buffalo grazed, then along the main road to Yangshuo, and the bus back to Guilin.

China Airways flew us back to Guangzhou. Work resumed. I joined the programme for training all the nurses in breathing exercises and vibration, and Dr. Wei worked his usual long hours. Sometimes I would watch him with Conrad bending over a patient, discussing the options. They were comrades too, in professional excellence. But not for long.

A few weeks later, waiting for Conrad in our tiny dining room, Mrs. Wong hovered around, wanting to bring in our dishes so she could get home to her grandson. As far as I could make out, her daughter worked night shift at a factory, so she had to start bicycling by 5:30 to get there in time. But where is Dr. Conrad? Why not bring it now, and I'll leave the tin covers on. Noodle soup, beef and greens, chicken in sauce, lots of rice and tea. At 5:40, he stormed in and plunked a sheaf of papers on the table, scraping the chair back to sit down.

"So what's up, Comrade?"

"Never mind. How was your day?"

"Good. Dr. Zhu gave me a year old baby with a severe club foot for splinting. Nurse Lai helped me, and the grandma, PoPo. She spoke mainly her village dialect so that was tricky. The baby was screaming which she really didn't like. Quite a struggle doing the fitting. But he was able to stand for the first time! PoPo was so thrilled. The baby looked so amazed: you should have seen his face! Then I watched Dr. Wei do electric acupuncture on an athetoid girl, and showed them some postural control activities." Conrad looked sceptical. "What's wrong? He doesn't always know if it will work, but it's worth a try."

"That's not what this says!" And he slapped the sheaf of papers. "He claims he's doing research. He showed me the abstract for this paper, for the conference in Shanghai last year. What a sham! 90% success rate, so he says!"

"Well, that's the only way he can get funding from the government for his department."

"So much for your wonderful Dr. Wei. I won't allow my credibility to be threatened by associating with such crap."

"Conrad! How can you say that? He told me at the banquet he's showing improvement of every degree, not a complete cure. He has to play the system or his programme will be squashed by the latest foreign marvel, like hyperbaric chambers or some crazy thing."

Conrad didn't bother restraining his contemptuous glance, to include me as well as Dr. Wei. He placed his chopsticks on his plate at a perfect perpendicular. "I've had it up to here with his manipulation. If this is representative, then the Chinese can forget being part of the world medical community."

"Don't be ridiculous! The government pervades everything! What about the children of black-listed parents who still can't go to university? If the wards don't do political propaganda every week, their pay gets cut. There's so many things we don't know about. We can't judge him."

"Marian, you're way out in left field. Where have you put the principles of our profession? You can't operate on wishing the patient to get better. You have to obtain clear evidence. For the rest of this project, I want you to adhere to physio association guidelines. We are both going to show these people that there's no compromise to ethical practice."

"Conrad, he doesn't want to compromise. He's fighting to get care for his patients. But he has to do it a different way."

"That's enough. We've bandied this around long enough." He stood up. Dismissed. We stacked the dishes in the cart for the morning staff and marched up stairs past the IV bottles and Chinese opera songs. I felt that my collar was too tight and he was pulling me on a leash.

My view of Dr. Wei took an entirely different track. He seemed to adjust himself to whoever came into his presence, so with no strain to himself he was just what everyone needed. He was dedicated to the care of children. He gave me the chance to explore all the types of paediatric practice in Guangzhou, and comment on what I saw. He seemed to enjoy looking at things through my eyes, and jotted down entries in his pocket notebook.

Next morning, Nurse Lai and I found the baby. We walked along the passageway from the residence, past the mail slots and the guard in her kiosk. We were earlier than usual because we'd offered to help Dr. Zhu in his clinic, taping children's club feet. We passed the metal teawater urns on the edge of the courtyard, and as we turned toward Outpatients, we heard a faint cry. Nurse Lai stopped me with a touch on my arm. And we paused to listen. It was barely audible above the workday commotion on Renmin Road outside. A weak, high-pitched cry. We followed it back to a wooden bench behind a water urn. The cry was coming from a bundle lying there. It was a living package left during the night. Nurse Lai lifted the outer layer and there was a tiny, distressed face. It was difficult to estimate the child's age: not newborn, but very fragile and small. Perhaps about four months old, but something was very wrong. It was breathing hard, crying in gasps, not loud, but worn out. The eyes couldn't focus well: they rolled upward to the left and there was some tremor. The little head was jerking to the left and the right hand was rigidly fisted and tight to the chest. Nurse Lai and I crouched over this pitiful bundle, the wrappings torn and patched. My hands were trembling and I began to shiver.

Nurse Lai reached out and enfolded the baby, gathering it up into her arms, rocking it to calm the heaving cries. Tears filled her black eyes and she looked at me with a wide, frightened stare. Instinctively I put my arm around her shoulder and we stayed like that, she tenderly looking down at the baby. Nurse Lai, young as she was, murmured comforting mothering sounds to the pinched little face. Finally I said, "We cannot leave him here. We must have him examined. Let's take him inside."

Nurse Lai said, "He is probably girl. Girl is more common to leave."

I propelled her back toward the inpatient wards. "Let's find Dr. Wei."

Nurse Lai became more composed. She clutched the bundle and marched up the grey cement steps to 3 North Neurology. Dr. Wei was in the middle of ward rounds, with Conrad there as well. We hung around on the edge and then I caught his eye. He took us in with a glance, and nodded a look to the small examining room behind the nurses' treatment room. We laid the baby on the table, and unwrapped him. Sure enough it was a girl, wet and soiled, and very thin. The skin was lax on her limbs, and her ribs were showing. Dr. Wei joined us, and then Conrad.

"Have you a little foundling here?" Dr. Wei asked us.

Nurse Lai explained in Guangdonghua. She tried to keep her voice professional, but she was a little angry. Dr. Wei just nodded, over and over, and all the while, gently tested the tiny thing for muscle tone and reflexes, listened to her lungs, looked in her eyes and ears, felt her abdomen, and then motioned to a staff nurse. She brought new blankets and a bottle of milk.

Nurse Lai tried to get her to suck on the nipple but it was difficult. Together we supported her head and stroked her cheeks and throat. Gradually the sobbing diminished and the baby tried feebly to suck. Dr. Wei turned to Conrad and me.

"You must be a little bit shocked."

We didn't answer. That showed we were.

"This happens from time to time. The family abandons their baby at the entrance to our hospital."

"Is there not some better system?" Conrad looked quite startled, but also steely cool.

Dr. Wei eyed him calmly. "It is quite effective, since the child will be looked after. There are many reasons for doing this."

Well. This is a Dr. Wei that I haven't seen yet: not apologizing to any Western expert. And not explaining either. "Dr. Wei, is it because the baby is handicapped?"

His kind tired eyes looked directly at me. "Yes, Miss Merry Ann, partly. We do not have facilities, except in the big cities, for specialized care. In many villages, all the adults must work all day very hard, and a child like this, requiring so much attention, is a drain on everyone. There are still prejudices too, as in your culture, against the handicapped. A family can be socially ostracized."

"Is there any progress being made?"

"Yes, Mr. Falk. We have a Child Welfare Institution, supported by the UN and donating sponsors, on the outskirts of the city. We take the foundlings there."

Nurse Lai joined in. "We call it the orphanage. Dr. Wei says I can accompany this baby today. Would you like to come?"

I quickly responded. "Oh yes. I would very much like to come." Conrad threw me a warning glance. Then I remembered Dr. Zhu. "But I must do Outpatient Clinic first."

Dr. Wei watched us and then made a suggestion, to make it more official. "Yes, we can book the van driver for the afternoon and have this as part of our community outreach programme. I have several residents who can cover for me. And possibly you, Mr. Falk, if you'd like to come."

Hmm. Is this a worthwhile idea? "I don't think so, Dr. Wei. My first priority must be to the continuity of my respiratory programme."

Oh come on, comrade. Your programme won't collapse in one afternoon. What's more important than the life of a child? Why do a mother and father abandon their child? Will they long to know what happened to their baby? What's it like to be left in a corner, in a crowded place, all alone? How does a little creature find a place to belong again? She cries for help, for one thing. And this tiny disabled child, in teaching Nurse Lai, and all of us, how to love, contributes as much as any foreign expert. The parents put her in the right place.

In the group gathered round the child, I realized Conrad was standing on one side by the door and the rest of us were on the other side, kind of clumped together. He was straight and tall, wavy hair carefully combed, tie perfect, lab coat clean with its fold creases still straight. It was odd, like watching a stranger. I know now I'll never belong in China, but that day I had the conviction that Dr. Wei and Nurse Lai were my real comrades, not Conrad.

"As you wish, Mr. Falk. We'll meet by the gates at one o'clock, if you change your mind. Nurse Lai, will you bring the child to the ward? Head Nurse Yi will find you a cot."

To myself, I called her Baby Michelle, after my old friend. The orphanage gave me a lot to think about. I still can't put that place or those children into a coherent category. The concept of a lost child is difficult to face. That idea, of being completely alone in the world, feels even closer to home right now. I wonder if Conrad will ever find the lost child inside himself, that child who learned about silence.

His silences with me gave out a message, as loudly as words: "I am very annoyed. I won't say why, however, because I want to punish you. You'll have to figure out what pleases me, and then you'll have the reward of my affection. Until then, my attention and acceptance of you is firmly withheld."

I can feel the tension in him, just recalling this. So I stare upward. This huge desert sky reminds me of the space in a Chinese painting, or the companionable quiet times with Dr. Wei: a space of peaceful emptiness to rest the eye and mind.

Conrad was a puzzle for Dr. Wei, as well as myself. One day in ICU he decided to use traditional medicine with a patient who wasn't responding to Western methods. As he held a moxibustion stick over an acupuncture point and the patient lay asleep, he explained the ancient five elements, the energy meridians that influence all our organ functions, and the balance of Yin and Yang. It sounded more like philosophy of nature than a science of medicine.

"All of us have Yin and Yang qualities, with shifts of emphasis and many shades that taken together reflect our balance of health. The Yin is the feminine, the moon, the cool, the reflective. The Yang is the masculine, the sun, the hot, the purposeful."

"This is interesting. Do you think I am balanced yet, in my Yin and Yang?"

He smiled reflectively. "I have only a short observation, Miss Merry Ann. Your past illness, the cancer, and the factors leading up to it, as well as the severe treatments you have undergone to combat it, have had a profound effect on your balance of qi. Your long efforts at nurturing others but not yourself have exhausted you. It is time to replenish your Yin, to rest and nurture yourself in a variety of ways."

I couldn't help asking, "How about Conrad?"

"Your friend is a complex person. It is instructive that he is so intensely focusing on his career. When a person such as Conrad holds his emotions close to his heart without expression, over time the basic flow of qi is constrained. This indicates an imbalance, possibly liver/fire rising, a Yang condition. There may also be some deeply embedded grief for which he has not yet found a resolution, but which he may regard as under control. It is important, however, not to presume too much about a person before we can safely say we understand the patterns of disharmony."

"It would be so good for him, if he could talk with you, Dr. Wei, and learn about these important concepts."

He looked a bit sceptical. "Perhaps. Thank you for your confidence in what I have to offer. The relationship between our body and our mind is very complex, as it is with each other. I do not think Mr. Falk has time to indulge in this exploration. I have observed that he is very clear in his mandate and does not deviate from it. I think Chinese ways do not hold any fascination for him".

For my last Sunday in China, we visited the Orchid Garden. Though Dr. Wei had been working several nights already and was quite exhausted, he insisted that I see the orchids, just coming into bloom. So we set off on the bus. This time we didn't need our jackets; the heat was already tropical by the middle of May. The garden was smaller than the others, and divided into sections. The orchids were in pots or hanging baskets. The white ones, with purple centres, were my favourites. Dr. Wei favoured the wine red ones, in big clusters. "My wife's name, 'Lan Fa,' means orchid. Naturally, it is my favourite flower. I'm sorry you have never met her. She comes home next month."

"That's great. You must be so happy about that."

"Yes. Shall we sit down for awhile?"

The air was misty and quiet under the trees, even though the big hotels and crowded main road were only a stone's throw away. We came to a pond, neatly edged with grass and irises, with a perfect reflection of a tiled pagoda. It was set before a bamboo grove: thick trunks of mustard yellow with random green stripes. Everything seemed designed to delight the eye.

Even a wall had inset tiles of dragons with coiling tails. Some late-blooming rhododendrons added a brilliant note of red in the reflection. At a shady spot, he sat down on the grass and leaned against a tree.

We talked about painting, how the painters show all the landscape at once, instead of by Western rules of perspective. And how each stroke has such meaning, the way the brush suggests bamboo or iris or plum blossom. It wasn't long before Dr. Wei's eyes closed and he lay with his head between two roots of the tree. I sat on, watching him breathe, until my own breath began to slow down, and rise and fall in concert with his. It seemed that this quiet man was leading me to a place of rest in my mind.

Of its own accord, my hand reached out and lightly rested on his forehead. The hovering lightness of this contact with him felt like a benediction. His gentle mind lay in repose within my palm and I felt my eyes close...

Smooth energy flows like currents of warm and cool water, through my hand and arm. It flows into my heart and around my breast, eddies round my back, down my legs to my feet. It flows upward through my pelvis, on into my lungs, through my other arm and my face and hair, and settles in a glow behind my eyes. I remain suspended and still, immersed in this glow. I am aware only of the glow. How can I describe it?

At last I opened my eyes and watched my hand on the sleeping face. My hand rose lightly away.

Dr. Wei opened his eyes and looked at me, and said, "Doh Jeh."

Thank you too, Dr. Wei.

Thinking about this experience, I am feeling it again. The heat, the car, the road through the desert, have lost their harshness. My solitude feels different now: I am happy deep inside.

Does this mean I am on the way to being whole again? I wonder if Dr. Wei realized what was happening between us. Did we support each other's qi? Will we always be able to do that, by thinking about it?

On our last day, we did a tour of the entire hospital to say good-bye. First there was the formal Directors' Meeting, when Dr. Huang, the Hospital Director, honoured Conrad with his speech likening him to Dr. Norman Bethune. While we were there, I heard later that Yuen, my electrical therapist comrade, had come to our rooms with her daughter, to meet me and give me the woollen shawl that she had made. So I missed saying farewell. That we recognized each other – that has to be enough. How did she know I would need her shawl? Many people gave us presents, warm smiles and handshakes. Then we had to leave Dr. Wei.

He smiled at me in his kind crinkly way. We looked at each other for the last time. We shook hands. My hand felt cool inside his. Even though I could feel the hard contour of his tendons and bones, his hand was very warm and enclosing. I wanted to stay there, resting. But I couldn't. I withdrew my hand. Joygin. Good-bye.

What was in that little bag I gave him was a teapot. What he gave me was a minaudière purse of beaded green and blue shaped like a frog, with a gold clasp and gold chain. He gave Conrad a book in a silk cover, about Chinese Rehabilitation.

From the plane window, I remember the Pearl River receding to a thread, the rice fields spreading out in tones of green and brown, and the high rises of Shen Zen becoming tiny blocks. Then for hours and hours, the blank blue Pacific. I stared at its vastness, in grief for the separation from what I had come to love. I didn't understand then, that all of China, including Dr. Wei, would come with me in my mind.

Conrad and I still had one more stop before I could get back to being a regular working mother: the conference. On the long flight he checked through all our notes, making sure everything was perfectly arranged. I studied the program: "North American Congress of Physiotherapy: Phoenix, Arizona. June 4-7, 1992." I flipped through the slate of dignitaries and speakers. There we were, large as life.

Past and future have almost come together. The rotations of time are overlapping. What seemed an endless unvarying plateau is giving way to hummocks of bushes. There is even the suggestion of a breeze in the shivering of the trees beside the road. The faint blue line of mountains has become a towering range of crags that dominates the horizon. At last, I'm leaving the desert behind.

PART FOUR

CEREMONY

"**H**i, folks. This is your captain speaking."
(Where am I? Where's the "chink, chink" of the bicycle bells in the street below my window? It's all puffy white clouds. What about the scrape of the garbage cans on Remnin Road? And the "cheep, cheep" of the sparrows, and the early morning exercise music? Conrad's beside me, but where's my hospital?) Ah yes, that's over.

"Your local time is now 6:15 am. We're beginning our descent into Phoenix. We'll be arriving at the terminal in approximately 37 minutes. It's a gorgeous day out there: clear skies, good visibility, already 64 degrees and light winds from the east. Thank you for flying with us. Enjoy your stay in Phoenix."

Hmm... A slight variant on this definition of gorgeous comes to mind: moist, misty, cool, tree shadows and mountain reflections. This land, however is shaping up flat and brown from my oval port-hole view. Ribs of pavement and strips of houses are accented by blue winks of swimming pools. Now industrial oblongs and business high-rises flash by, and the jet beast exhales as we brake on the runway. As we thump over each crack in the concrete squares on the approach to the terminal, I turn to my comrade Conrad to speak, but his face stops me. He looks so relieved, so satisfied: he's pulled it off. He looks as if a weight has been lifted off him. His face looks thinner than when we started out, and his eyes paler and more inward-looking. He is more remote from me than ever before. And his project is successfully almost complete, whereas mine is still lingering in the process.

After the no man's land of customs and baggage ("where's my declaration form? I know I put it somewhere." "Marian, try your pocket." "Oh yeah. Right.") we drag our luggage through the automatic doors to the taxi stand. Whoo. The air hits us, hot and dry. My throat and lungs are taken aback. So are my eyes. The people on the sidewalk look reversed: like a photo negative, their skin is dark but their hair is pale. The really remarkable thing is their pale eyes, with black pupils so round. Conrad flags down a cab and we're off, through wide streets. Cars are everywhere, all different kinds, and no black bicycles. No cyclists straining with loads of concrete pipe, no bamboo scaffolding, no one brushing their teeth over a drain, no farmer reaching for a tuft of choice grass from a ditch bank for his water buffalo, no ditches. At least there are palm trees. And most of the signs, I can read. Some in Spanish. So many restaurants, and huge low buildings with acres of parking lots instead of fields or markets. Everything seems scattered outward and magnified.

We navigate out of the city and head for the resort and convention centre. Before long we've left the warehouses and the rubbish clinging to chain link fences and the freeway opens onto a wide view of desert and sky. The bleached land is a shock at first. A line of blue mountains in the East is a relief to the eyes. At last, "Oasis Resort" appears ahead of us and we drive along an avenue of cactuses until we come to a hacienda of adobe with red tiled roof and the incongruous sound of splashing water. Spanish-style wrought iron twirls like vines on bannisters and balconies, flamboyant tropical trees stand in pots on the veranda and a bank of marble steps leads to the entrance. Lights are glittering everywhere. Tall slender people in white and pale caramel clothes waft around. This place is like a mirage.

We stand amidst our pile of bags until a bellhop whisks them onto a cart, and Conrad remarks with a smile, "At last, back to civilization."

"Conrad, we can't stay here."

"Why ever not?"

"It's horrible. It's so rich."

"Marian, I'll register at the desk. You sit here with the bags. We'll discuss it later."

It's no good. I can't stand this. A power-suited woman clicks by, eyeing me up and down. I feel like an alien in a space suit. Or the beaver in Qing Ping Market.

"All right. We're booked in, to adjoining rooms. The reception's not until 7 tonight. So we'll have time to get our bearings."

"Could we go somewhere simpler? Somewhere real?"

Narrowing eyes and mouth. Narrowing appraisal. "You're in a spot of culture shock, it would appear. I'll ask the concierge for a car and suggestions for an outing. Come on, let's get settled in."

"Okay. I guess so."

No escape. The room, with its remote control this and that, looks out onto a pool fed from a waterfall springing miraculously from carefully placed boulders. Carefully placed golden-coloured people are sipping drinks from a poolside bar. The phone rings. It's him.

"Ready?"

"Yes."

"Okay, meet you in the hall."

Good idea, the car. He hands me a map with a circle around an area in the south.

"There's a nature preserve, she said, with some trails and a good view from the top. Have you pulled yourself together?"

"Yeah. I guess you're right… it must be jetlag. It'll be great to stretch our legs at last."

So we head out to the country in the white rental car, Conrad driving. We leave the glitz behind. What about food? I'm so hungry. We're coming to a big intersection on the highway. A huge semi-trailer idles beside us. Here's a sprawling strip mall. That should have something to eat. Talk about choice. Packages of chips, cereal, cookies, pop, etc. etc. Where's the food? No shrimp balls, no bok choy, no chrysanthemum tea. I hunt and hunt and because he's going into that stony, exasperated silence, I grab some bread and oranges, juice and a package of something that looks like nuts.

At last we seem to be getting somewhere. There's the turnoff on the map, winding through a formation of jagged reddish cliffs.

"Conrad, I've got my tapes in the backpack. Do you mind if I put on some music?"

"Go ahead."

Ahh. Good old Leon Russell, flamenco guitar, a spot of blues. I made these tapes for the car at home when I'm tangled up in rush hour traffic. They help me get my head sorted out – a nostalgia trip. Oops. His face is that stony mask again. What's wrong? The music? Probably thinking about his speech.

Well, here's a surprise! A lovely Spanish-looking village: no neon signs, no trucks, not many people. And there's a cappuccino bar across from the central square.

"Con, let's stop."

"What for?"

"Let's take a coffee break. This is beautiful, like Spain. Let's relax in the sun a bit."

"Just a bit. We don't have much time."

What I mean is, let's get out of this car, out of this close space that's beginning to get smaller and smaller. Let's recapture how it used to be. But he doesn't want coffee. He decides to look for postcards instead.

It's a delight to sit alone at the table, I must admit, and expand my senses toward this surprising moment. Turn a corner, and here's a new world. I'm remembering Madrid, how the old men also sat for hours with their tiny espressos, on the sunny side of the Plaza Mayor. Such excitement, to see everything, but now, I'm lingering over moments like this. I see him striding across the square, between the palm trees and two children with their mothers. His expression is closed to me, still a mask. It's definitely time to move on. I drive this time. I concentrate on breathing, to keep this sunny moment a little longer.

A signpost notifies us, we're nearing the nature preserve: cactus heaven. I turn the car onto a twisting gravel road, among hills of tall cactuses. Just beyond is a staircase of burnt sienna rock ranged in an uneven line across the sky. A circular hole in one rock face creates a blue eye beaming down on the pulsing heat. Black shadows define the facets of stone, but in the valleys the light is unrelieved. The cactuses reach and writhe their long spiky limbs.

I stop the car under the speckled shade of a twig shelter. We step out, shade our eyes as we look around: it's stark, sharp and devoid of colour. At first. We stuff our cameras and the food into my backpack and pick our way up the slope, avoiding the needly plants. Gradually I become aware of what's there: the grey-green century plants shading into purple, rust, lemon, indigo. Lime-green clusters of cactus stems like large zucchinis are fringed by black and vermilion-red spikes. I pull out my camera. A group of lumpy cactuses between my lens and the sun take on the illusion of softness, each with an aureole of gold like a buddha. I raise my lens to include Conrad in the picture but I see no softness there. His long legs in brown pants are straight, angular. His head is turned away, expression remote and concentrated, like a student before a test. Again I have the sense of viewing a stranger.

It's searingly hot. I watch his long legs ahead on the trail and follow like King Wenceslas' page. But an inferno of heat takes over: the usual hot flushes that have dogged me since chemotherapy days.

I feel flames rising to my head, and sweat beading everywhere; even my ankles are sweating. My lungs can't cope, in spite of my panting. My throat is desiccating. My heart is running in circles. I sink down on a rock. Head on knees. Just breathe and throb.

I drift into that place that feels so real at the time but is only a dream. I'm still trudging along a path but I'm back to being a frog and he's a deer, straining to get ahead. I'm small and green but fading fast. I croak but he doesn't answer. We're held together by a string but he's pulling at it and his brown legs are stepping too fast. This is very dangerous for me; if I keep up this pace I will die. I don't want to walk down this path any more. I don't know where it's leading. I want to walk on my own path. That way I'd know where I'm going. I can feel my greenness fading into grey and my limbs are disappearing and I'm becoming scaly and slit-eyed and slithery. With thin tongue and fangs. That bite him in his brown leg. That sever the string that binds us. He kicks me, and with deer leaps, bounds away and I am lying bleeding in the dust. Breathing in the dust. I sense a shadow over me, and look up to see him.

"What's wrong?"

"Oh. Just resting a bit."

"I thought it was you who was the mountaineer."

"Not any more, I guess."

"Well, we won't have time to go to the top now. We'd better go back to the shelter for lunch." When am I ever going to see the real person behind his mask? What's he thinking – that I'm a klutz, a millstone that he has to drag around again, a tedious child?

We sit in silence at the table under the shelter, watching a bird flicking its tail on a spiky perch. I throw some shreds of bread that it pecks at but doesn't eat, until I notice him shaking his head and staring at a small notice, "Do <u>not</u> feed the wildlife." He turns away from me, shows me his very straight, rigid spine, and drinks from a box of juice. Oh brother. I have transgressed, it seems in every possible way.

"I'm sorry, Conrad. I guess I don't have the stamina I used to."

He turns slightly, acknowledging that he's heard me.

"Conrad, I don't know if I should say this. Things seem very shaky between us. Maybe we should start over again."

A shrug. He stands up. "I don't think so. Hashing over the old territory would just make things more intolerable. On what basis would we start anything new?"

Our eyes meet for a painful instant before his slide on to scan the parched landscape.

"You've changed, Marian. Somehow I have to deal with that."

"Conrad, we've been…"

But he shakes his head and turns from me, back down toward the car. We descend to a low place where there's little hope, where our silence is weighted down, heavy with all our unspoken words. We drive down the gravel road to the highway and back toward the resort.

I should have been able to brush aside the silence of that journey. But for some reason it gathered intensity instead of melting away. It was poisonous. It exuded judgement and frustration and fear. I tried breathing, visualizing peaceful waves washing in and out, but the result was that blubbering outburst that stopped the car on the side of the road. It was so embarrassing, crying like that and not being able to say anything. And Conrad not saying anything. The only relief was the setting sun, on its way back to China. If only I could have been going back too, to where I belonged. Magenta clouds exploded behind the jagged black hills in the west. They rushed to meet the moon, serene and pearly, that hung in the east, over the beckoning line of mountains. Even at such a distance, in muted blue and mauve, their sharp peaks piled into a dramatic event. They invited me to reach toward them, toward cool air and freedom.

I thought, watching that, "I just can't seem to keep things in or sweep them under like I used to. I don't have the energy or the inclination to stand on my head for approval, to rack my brains for the way to please him. I want to shed my old ways and go somewhere else. What is it he needs– my devotion forever?"

There was nothing for it but to carry on. We arrived at the reception a little late but that didn't matter. I would have been happy to skip the whole thing. It was not a thrill to be introduced to all his compatriots from across North America. I was still blushing up in waves of perspiration, or was it shame – quite unseemly in a brocade-draped room of casual elegance. Put me back in a room cramped with white iron cribs with peeling paint from the spring rains blown in from the window, and Chinese moms and kids sharing soup and swapping stories with the families across the beds.

Sink or swim. Swim or not swim. Not with these cold fish. It was easy to slip away, sit by the ornamental pool, stare into the water and plants highlighted by flickering mushroom lights. Easy to slip into an illusion of moist peace. To imagine the syncopated chorus of frogs and the squish of saturated moss under my feet. To inhale and exhale, to quench my thirst for calm. Waves of light gathering and falling away in my forehead. Light and dark. Light and dark. Gentle murmurings. Water gurgling. Suspension. Happiness seeping in. It's going to be all right. We were partners in something wonderful, something that will always be with us. When I returned to the reception, he was animated, immersed in effusive chat with his tongsi. Ignored, I was a distant observer. But temporarily happy.

Presentation Day at last. Notes in hand. Slides at the ready.

A slight glitch: "Oh no, Marian. Not your little green Mao suit."

"If it's good enough for Dr. Yao, it's good enough for these people." So there.

We sit on the speakers' platform, respectfully absorbing the other presenters' thoughts: The Future of Evidence-based Practice, Protocols for Treating Traumatic Sports Injuries, New Advances in Splinting the Burned Hand. And then us.

He stands at the podium in his beautifully-cut navy blue suit, looking from the height of his professional excellence out towards the circles of bright light and the rows of waiting faces. Some are eager, new to the game. Others are seasoned troopers, conscientious contributors to our profession. The wild cards are there, on the lookout for old partners in crime. So are the new breed of up-to date managers, efficient with computers on their laps.

He begins, telling everyone about this pioneering work of ours, bringing the West to these health care clients of emerging, beleaguered China. He motions to the A-V person to start the slides. Suddenly, we're back in Guangzhou. There's Nurse Lai at the entrance, by the bicycle racks, with Renmin Road jostling by. There are the Outpatient nurses, waving at us through the sea of waiting families, everyone in coats because there's no heating system. Oh, there's Dr. Zhu examining the boy with Legg-Perthes disease, whose only treatment could be his father carrying him for six months because his work unit couldn't pay. The familiar door to ICU, scraped at the bottom from all the carts pushing through, is open. There's Baby Wu Bak Wing wrapped in his thick red quilt, sleeping in his oxygen tent. The staff in the post-surgical room are lined up smiling at us with the donated equipment prominently displayed. And there's Conrad at the Directors' Meeting with Nurse Lai translating our plan for introducing Rehab to the Guangzhou People's General Hospital. And there's one of me making a nest for an incubated premature baby. I look fluffy, like a sheep, next to the sleek black-haired nurses, but stuck right in and happy. There's no picture of Yuen; he didn't catch her.

Suddenly Dr. Wei is looking at us, with his hand on a very sick cardiac patient connected by a myriad of wires to the monitor. Did Conrad take that photo? Dr. Wei looks interrupted, as if he doesn't have time for this. I am startled to see an expression on his face that I have never seen before: he looks so vulnerable, but the word defiant also jumps into my mind, almost as if he is protecting his patient from us. This image evokes the memory of the patriot in Goya's painting of the massacre in Madrid. Oh Dr. Wei, you are following in your father's footsteps. What did Conrad say, that made you look like this? More slides flash by, but it's hard to concentrate.

At last he's summing up, and acknowledging the applause. "And now I'd like to give you Marian Zabiuk, who will describe in more detail the Paediatric Programme that we established."

So I'm standing there. I realize my notes are still behind me, under the chair. It doesn't matter. I don't want to say that anyway.

"I love these people. I feel so honoured that they accepted me into their lives. They cared for me in a way that I have not encountered in the West. It is so presumptuous to tell them what to do. We were aliens but they trusted that we came with good will. They deserve the greatest respect for surviving through the hardships that they have endured for so long. What they don't need is competitive, aggressive attitudes that will pit the people against each other. Why can't we support them to grow how they wish, and encourage them to give us their riches, meaning their humanity and wisdom? I feel so grateful that they could forgive our brashness in forcing ourselves upon them, and I hope that we did the least damage possible, and gave them some warm memories to sustain them in their care of their patients. I want you to love them too. If you could feel the warmth of these people coming across to you from so far away, then you could be healed by them. And that is the first thing you need to do."

I am quite overcome. My heart has a terrible pain, yearning for my lost people, who are so present in this room. The tragedy of separation, the horror of cruelty through misunderstanding, that has plagued the human world for so many centuries, is an unbearable thought. The futility of trying to convey my feeling, my unattainable desire for making the happy union of all our peoples, carries a note of anger, to protect my Chinese loved ones from harm by the West. I become aware that I am standing at the podium, but saying nothing. Only crying. So I sit down again. Conrad leaps up to give a conclusion and announce the arrangements for lunch. As he passes me leaving the stage, he leans over and snaps, "Marian, that was appalling." And off he goes.

I've got to pull the car over to the side of the road. I've decided to write to Conrad, one more time. I don't have long, before this journey ends.

Dear Conrad,
So. I've disgraced you. What you and those others wanted was for me to be professional, that is, discreet and predictable. But that's the old way of trying to please. It's dangerous for me, Conrad, repressing what I really think and feel. Maybe that's part of why I got sick. So embarrassing or not, I won't be bowing to the authority of your silence, or your direction on how to act. Because I want so much to live. I'll be by myself but it won't be like before. I'll use what I've learned up till now, on this journey, and act in the world according to my own perspective.

All along this road, it seemed that I was the rejected one, but I haven't looked at what was happening to you. Over the years I've known you, you must have come to terms with not living a regular married life like me, not being able to meet your parents' expectations, not being able to talk about your fears openly. You've created an honest dignified life for yourself and I have no idea how you accomplished that, because I never asked.

All along there have been clues of how much I've meant to you but I haven't paid enough attention. Thinking back, a big ingredient in your love for me was your compassion. Outside the Prado, after looking at Goya's Black Paintings, you crossed over the line for me; you almost sacrificed who you really were so I would be happy. I didn't understand what that gift must have cost you at that moment, even if you had to take yourself back. And when you invited me to China, sure, it was to take my mind off cancer, but it was more. It was hope – hope that we would be partners again. You needed me just to be with. You trusted me to be equal to the reputation you've built up for so many years. Your good name as a therapist, teacher and expert has been your path to self-respect and dignity.

And I spat in your face with my speech. I rejected your achievement in fulfilling your goal with the UN, by demeaning the Western approach before all those people. I stomped on your values of excellence in our profession the way it's evolved since the 60's. If you were Chinese, I'd say I'd made you lose face. And you didn't deserve that. You just weren't emotionally involved in China like I was. Maybe you even envied how involved I was with my comrades. Maybe you were watching me enjoying myself, while I regained my joie de vivre, as you'd planned. Going to China was your alternative treatment for me. And it worked. But too well. I concentrated so much on my Chinese community, especially Dr. Wei, that I began pulling away from you. It looked as if I wasn't loyal to your expectation of our partnership.

Simply put, I'll say that you've loved me all these years. Our friendship didn't have a chance to deepen, and now it's all disintegrated. I'm so sorry. Please forgive me. I didn't realize that you needed me; I thought you were self-sufficient. The irritable remarks you made about Dr. Wei were messages of pain, of jealousy, of feeling discarded – why didn't I see that? I didn't take the trouble to reach out toward you. That speech really was the final straw. All you needed was a mild echo of your message to our audience. You'd say that I wouldn't understand… but I do now.

Now you're alone in your loss as much as I am. It'll take a lot of healing now, for you to let it all go. The best thing I can do is stay away. And acknowledge the compliment that you chose me several times as your companion.

Dear friend, I hope that wherever you are at this moment, you can find some place to rest from all this. One day my name won't bring jabs of pain; I'll just be an episode, or a curious item in your collection of antiques: curiosities no longer useful, to be lined up on the back shelf gathering dust. Then you'll be able to nod in amusement, "Ah yes, that Marian...I once knew her." And you'll be healed. Thank you, Conrad, for all you gave me, know it or not. The damage we've done to each other will be repaired by ourselves. Conrad, this really is goodbye.

With love,
Marian

I put my letter at the end of the conference notes, and slid them onto the back seat. I turned the key in the ignition and swung the car again onto the empty straight road heading east.

There was a left turn off the highway onto a gravel road, after the sign "National Park – Geronimo's Last Stand." The track wound upward through a long narrow valley, past an old log house with a phone on the side wall. I guess it was a ranger station. I tried calling Mum and the kids but there was no answer. Driving deeper into the valley, I became surrounded by steep rock walls, rising dark and cracked to the top where rounded boulders were piled up like giant heads. They seemed gouged and bleeding because the stone was stained a purplish red. The wind blew through them like the whining and cracks of arrows and guns, the groaning and crying of the dying warriors, the panicked neighing of horses, and the rushing mocassined feet of the wailing women.

I stopped the car in a dry grassy meadow and fished out some stuff from my backpack: an orange, some matches, my mother's coat and Yuen's shawl, my frog purse and the jar with curving lid.

There was a faint path through the grass to a dry river-bed edged with a tall procession of trees – huge birches with that white bark flecked with dashes, and shivering leaves. Some way along there was a flat clearing of sand and dry leaves. It was so hot even under the trees that I had to sit down. The air was still and quiet then. The sorrowful battle of the wind had faded away. I ate my orange and then I just sat on the sand for I don't know how long. Such fatigue. It was as if my body had just shut down. But around me I had a sense of shadowy figures. They drifted closer. Phantoms...

My father's wearing his fedora and plaid shirt, and he's carrying his map of the back country. He says, "You have many stories still to tell." Shep's walking beside him, and even though he's a shadow dog his fur is all the colours of the earth and he looks unblinking at me.

My mother has her silvery hair wound up in a chignon like she used to do and she's wearing her pink jogging suit. She's talking softly, making up her grocery list: "walnuts, baking soda, brown sugar, oatmeal, lemons, eggs. Marian, you'll always be my child. Now I need help getting everything done."

And Josef is here. He's wearing the old ski sweater that he would never give up, that would collect little snow baubles on the edge when he took his flying jumps and wiped out. He's carrying his saw and he whispers to me, "I'll always be waiting, Doll. You know that."

Behind him come Emily and Hans holding Connie's hands between them.

They've all got shorts and tank tops on for the summer and their fresh wide eyes smile at me with such love. "Don't leave us yet. We still need you."

Along comes Michelle in her cream velour dressing gown carrying a tray of vegetarian lasagne. She says something curious, "Memory is enough, Marian. You don't have to go on and on."

Dr. Wei is very pale in his rumpled lab coat but his eyes shine black from behind his round glasses and he carries a moxibustion stick. He tells me, "Our ways of healing are always available for us."

Finally a native woman with wispy grey hair slowly circles around, wrapped in a grey blanket and carrying a long feather. Her voice is slow and sad. "I cry for my dead warriors. I cry for the children unborn. I will teach you how to grieve. The earth is our temple, lit by the sun and the moon. We submit to its laws, and find joy over and over."

I feel enclosed and protected. These shadows are the village of my heart. They gradually fade away and I see this sandy place with a clear purpose. I have to bury my friendship.

So I stand up and pull my frog purse out of the backpack. I take from it the beaded earrings that I got at the powwow and put them on. I tear off two strips of paper from my flight boarding pass and find a blackened stick and write "Marian" and "Conrad" on them. I put them in the Creek Pottery jar and lift it onto the sand. Then I dig with my hands a hole about the size of a washbasin and place the jar in the bottom. It lies there, jewel-coloured like the eye in a peacock feather, or a june bug, or an abalone shell brought up to the light for a moment. I cover it with sticks and dry leaves and then round river stones until I have a rounded mound. I light some matches and stick them inside the mound and blow until there's smoke and flames. As I stand looking at the fire I've made, I breathe in the smoke and feel my sorrow, for the friendship that I've lost, just overwhelm me. I begin rocking and then begin to stumble around the mound. Gradually I feel myself rotating and gently swinging my body and limbs this way and that. This ritual carries me along, into a private place of certainty…

The smoke is coming from times long past. It is the spirit of the earth and its creatures telling me that the earth absorbs all things and I can leave this buried grief and walk forward out into the open again. It is also the spirit of the air that invisibly sustains us in every moment, that gives us all freedom to look around at everything anew, for the birds to fly free, and for Conrad to fly free of me. His freedom and mine. The smoke is the spirit of fire, the heart of our feelings that burned us but gave us warmth for so many years. The heat of my love for Conrad is still here, even in our loss. And last of all the smoke is the spirit of water, the element that washes us clean and cools our fever, that drowns us and revives us and expresses our pain in tears that pool to give us our reflection. Even though in this dry place water is only a memory, that memory gives me hope. I can believe in the farewell and he can become a memory. So can I. We can both start again by ourselves.

I don't know how long it's been, since the smoky mound's been cool. The colours of the setting sun are almost gone. So I'm walking back to the meadow and I'm lying down, with my mother's coat and Yuen's shawl wrapped around me. When I wake up, the stars are like you wouldn't believe: thousands of sparks from my fire. I stand in the valley in the starlit darkness like I'm being born.

The moon slips up over the knobbly crown of the valley wall. As I turn to look behind me, I see the bear and then I realize – it's my own shadow. When I turn again to look at the moon I've decided: the bear of death will always be following me, not confronting me. I'm the leader now. Walking towards the light. Death is in the background.

The car is waiting in the meadow. It's simple finding my way back onto the highway. The sky gradually lightens and the line of mountains recedes in the rearview mirror. Here's a straight stretch of road through flat fields dotted with cactuses. I stop the car to watch the sun rise. A bird has just landed on a fencepost in front of me and is beginning to sing to the dawn. Its beak, needle sharp, is wide open like scissors. But its pulsing throat is soft and swelling with the cascading notes of its song.

At last here's the glow of the sun on my face. My skin feels washed and shining. It's peaceful being alone, and knowing I'm almost home.

Photo: Colin Mahony

Born in Vancouver Canada, Carol May has lived in diverse landscapes. She explores these through writing, painting and photography. She lives now in Vancouver and Hornby Island, BC. Desert Journey is her first novel.

ISBN 1412037b7-0